He didn't belong here

Sean was honest enough to admit that to himself.
He was country-born and country-bred—and
liked it that way. He didn't mind making a
donation of his time to charity—as a volunteer
fireman he'd done plenty of that. But he didn't
like drawing attention to himself, didn't like
standing on stage, *didn't* like auctioning himself
off like a side of beef. He was a simple man,
preferring his relationships with women to be
intimate and private.

Sighing, he prayed that this evening would end
soon—and as painlessly as possible. Sean was
about to make his way inside the auction room
when he was struck by an unusual sight. A
woman stood just outside the exit, her back
braced against the concrete wall, her coat open
to the winter's breeze. She was watching him—
not in that curious oh-my-gosh-is-it-really-him
way, but more of a sensual summing up. Her eyes
raked over him from head to toe and she spoke.

"I wouldn't go in there if I were you."

Dear Reader,

Have you ever faced a New Year's Eve without a date? If you have, you'll understand why Dana and her friend Elise decide the best way to get a date is to *buy* a guy! But with the studly "New Year's Bachelors," these two women get more than they bargained for!

Be sure you don't miss the companion novel to this one—*Elise & the Hotshot Lawyer* by Emily Dalton—coming to you next month.

Ring in the New Year with the "New Year's Bachelors"!

Happy reading,

Debra Matteucci
Senior Editor & Editorial Coordinator
Harlequin Books
300 East 42nd Street
New York, NY 10017

Lisa Bingham

DANA AND THE CALENDAR MAN

Harlequin Books

TORONTO • NEW YORK • LONDON
AMSTERDAM • PARIS • SYDNEY • HAMBURG
STOCKHOLM • ATHENS • TOKYO • MILAN
MADRID • WARSAW • BUDAPEST • AUCKLAND

To the best critique group in the world.
Thanks for the
all-night brainstorming sessions,
scores of "artsy-fartsy" movies
and all the hours of infinite understanding

ISBN 0-373-16662-1

DANA AND THE CALENDAR MAN

Chapter One

"Ladies! Welcome to the sixth annual Celebrity Bachelor Auction, sponsored by the Make a Wish Foundation!"

A round of raucous applause greeted the female disc jockey who was serving as the emcee for the evening.

Dana Shaw clapped, as well, gazing around her in amazement at some of the audience members who were jumping from their seats and whistling.

"Can you believe this response?" she murmured under her breath, leaning close to Elise Allen's ear so that she could be heard over the din.

Elise merely shrugged.

In all honesty, Dana would have to say that neither she nor Elise had been prepared for the air of frivolity that permeated the ballroom of the Red Lion Hotel. They'd come to this affair on the spur of the moment after meeting for lunch at Dana's apart-

ment. As was their habit every year on New Year's
Eve, the two women, old college roommates, had
met at noon for a quiet party before parting to
whatever escorts and activities awaited them for the
evening. This year, neither of them had made plans
for later—neither of them had even had...

Dates.

Dates.

"Damn," Dana whispered under her breath,
wondering if she'd have time to make a quick call on
her cellular phone before the auction began. Reaching for the voluminous shoulder bag she invariably
carried everywhere she went, she began to rummage
through the contents.

Seeing her sudden inattention to the proceedings
onstage, Elise leaned across the table to whisper,
"What's wrong?"

"Fred."

"Fred?" Elise echoed, then fixed Dana with an
accusatory stare. "You didn't leave him in your
apartment, did you?"

Dana scrambled to think. Fred Wallaby, a shy little man of about forty-five, had been left on her
doorstep—quite literally—just before Elise had arrived. One of her aunts had sent him as a blind date
for the evening. When Dana had explained she had
company for the afternoon, he'd timidly said he'd
wait. Unwilling to cause a scene, she'd sent him into

the study with some hors d'oeuvres and told him to help himself to the supply of videos she had on hand.

She sighed. Fred was merely another candidate in a long line of prospective suitors her aunts had sent her way in the hopes that they could spark some sort of romance. They just didn't seem to understand that Dana wasn't currently interested in finding a mate. At the moment, she was married to her career—and she liked it that way. When she felt lonely or in need of an evening out, there were plenty of men in her acquaintance willing to volunteer as an escort. She didn't need a trio of elderly women sending in her direction every Tom, Dick and Harry they encountered on the street.

"Didn't Fred leave with us?" Elise asked, dragging Dana's thoughts back to the matter at hand.

Dana shrugged. "The last I saw of him, he was munching on a cheese ball and watching a Doris Day movie. *Pillow Talk*," she clarified absentmindedly, racking her brain to remember what had occurred those last few hectic minutes in her apartment. "I think I set the burglar alarm," she mumbled, "but I don't remember if I saw him go."

Elise chuckled openly.

"Stop it! It isn't funny." Shaking her head, Dana said firmly, "No. I'm sure he's gone. I think I remember ushering him outside. We were in a bit of a rush, but..."

Rush didn't even begin to explain it. She and Elise had spent a glum hour in Dana's living room, mourning the death of Dolores "Dottie" Montgomery—the woman who had served as their landlady and surrogate mother during their years at the University of Utah. They'd roomed together in her sprawling bungalow in the Avenues, sharing with the woman their secrets, their triumphs, their pain. It had been difficult to resign themselves to her passing.

When their lunch had been interrupted by a UPS deliveryman toting a note from Dottie—dated months before her death—two pastel envelopes and two tickets to this bachelor auction, they'd been stunned to discover Dottie had included them in her will. She'd left each of them one thousand dollars, with the command that they spend it on something frivolous and impulsive. No car payments or bills. Whatever they purchased was to give them pleasure.

The fact that Dottie had also included the bachelor-auction tickets had not been lost on Dana. She knew it was the sweet old woman's way of communicating to them from beyond the grave, encouraging them to get on with their lives, to include a little romance and adventure in their humdrum existences. With Elise divorced and Dana fast becoming an old maid, Dottie had thought the time had come for them both to indulge in what she called some "spice."

When Elise had proved a little hesitant about the evening, it was Dana who'd slapped the tickets on the table and encouraged, "Come on, girlfriend. Let's go shopping, get ourselves all dolled up, then buy ourselves a man!"

The statement might have sounded outrageous to anyone who didn't know her, but Elise had gone along. More than that, she'd understood the motivation that lay behind Dana's suggestion—known Dana had had enough of her aunts' constant matchmaking and wanted to provide her own escort for the birthday celebration she'd been suckered into attending later that week. To get herself a *man*. Not a "companion," not a "friend," not even a "knight in shining armor." She needed someone big, strong, handsome and totally earth-shattering. Someone with an air of danger and an aura of mystique who would convince her aunts that she'd had her fill of "nice" fellows with "nice" manners. It was the only way to show the three older women that their choices in blind dates over the past few years had not been completely welcome—nor had they been all that tempting.

She needed someone like...

"Ladies, I'm afraid our first bachelor of the evening will be a few minutes late due to icy conditions on I-15, but we thought we'd let you know he was on his way. You've all seen him, you've all heard of him. He's none other that Sean O'Malley—Mr. January from the 1995 Volunteer of the Month Calendar!"

The emcee held up a glossy calendar, displaying a ruggedly handsome man wearing little more than a pair of suspenders and the bottom half to his bunker gear. Even at a distance, his dark hair and intense indigo eyes were clearly discernible. The cheers and wolf whistles reached new and earsplitting heights.

"It looks as if I don't need to remind you how *that* particular publication took the state by storm when..."

Sean O'Malley.

Sean O'Malley?

Dana sat straighter in her seat, craning to see the photograph being held high for the gawking audience.

"Here's a man who knows how to light a fire and could stoke the coals so they burn white-hot!" the woman at the podium continued.

Dana listened with half an ear. Her skin began to tingle, her heart to race. Although she was sure she wasn't the only woman in the room to entertain such reactions, she was positive her reason was unique. O'Malley was overtly handsome, to be sure, the sort that would give any woman a case of tummy flut-

ters. But Dana was attracted to him in an entirely
different way. He was the same man she'd been trying to interview for months. Twelve long months.
Ever since she'd walked into the editing room at
Channel 9 and seen his photograph hanging from the
production bulletin board.

"Isn't that the one—?" Elise began.

"Yes," Dana interrupted, already scrambling for
her bidding paddle. But when she heard the emcee
saying, "He'll know just how to heat up those cold
winter nights," she dropped it again, her fingers becoming unaccountably clumsy.

He was the sort that dreams were made of. Every
woman's fantasy, there, in the flesh. That was why
she'd wanted to find him, why she'd wanted to interview him. His notoriety over the past year had
come out of nowhere, but what had increased the
interest in his background, made him the hottest
topic in the intermountain West, was that no one really knew anything about him other than that he
served on the volunteer fire department in a small
community in Cache Valley, southwest of Logan. If
Dana could discover more about the man behind the
myth, so to speak, she would have one of the hottest
projects for her station's "Utah People" segment,
which aired each Sunday afternoon. It might even be
"sexy" enough to attract nationwide attention.

She leaned toward Elise, trying to keep her voice as low as possible but unable to control her eagerness. "What does it say in the catalog? What is this man offering?"

Elise quickly thumbed through the list of men and the services they'd offered, then shrugged. "A week of entertainment—" she grinned and caught Dana's eye "—buyer's choice."

A week. *A week.* The hairs at the back of her neck were standing at attention now. Finally, fate had winked her way. Her aunts' party was scheduled for this weekend, with the ball the culminating event on Saturday night. Even though Dana was officially on vacation for the next few days in order to attend the lavish event, she could easily snag a camera crew and have them meet her at her aunts' retirement village. She could highlight the charity-auction angle—how Sean O'Malley, one of the most elusive bachelors in the state—was sacrificing his time to help little children in need. Maybe she could even move up the date of her upcoming project, "Creative Dating in the Nineties," and tie this piece in as the last segment.

Yes. Yes!

The more she thought about the idea, the more she liked it. Seven full days. She could get an in-depth interview, lots of tape, real quality stuff. In the meantime, she'd have an escort for the grand hoopla her aunts had planned. She'd knock their socks off with an escort like this. They wouldn't dare line her up with another living soul for months. Years.

"I'm going to have him," she muttered under her breath. "He's mine."

"You'll have your work cut out for you," Elise commented, surveying the interest this particular bachelor had inspired in the audience around them.

"I don't care. I've got to have an incredible date for that damn ball my aunts have planned. Otherwise, they'll line me up with some fifty-year-old virgin who lives with his mother. You wait and see."

"There will be others to bid on who will be just as good-looking," Elise began, but Dana shook her head.

"No. It has to be O'Malley. Not only is he perfect for the party, but I want this man for an interview. He's just what I'm looking for. Someone mysterious. Someone close lipped and intriguing. Someone who will attract the attention of—"

"Five hundred dollars!" a voice yelled out.

As soon as she heard the bid, Dana glared at a cool blonde seated at the table next to them. The crowd oohed and aahed at the startling offer when the bachelor in question hadn't even arrived yet.

Dana's eyes narrowed as she realized the person who'd cried out was none other than Jeanine Rush, a reporter recently hired by a competing station.

"Just what does she think *she's* doing?" Dana whispered, leaning forward and staring at her competition—not just in the bidding but in the news game, as well. The more she stared at the woman, the firmer her resolve grew. She assumed that Jeanine had bid on O'Malley for the same reason she had. To force an interview with a man who had previously been mysteriously silent with the press.

"No way," Dana muttered under her breath, not about to be bested by some platinum-haired...*child* who barely finished college.

It was obvious that Jeanine had recognized Dana. Her smug smile was all-knowing. She might have been in the area little more than a year, but she knew Dana Shaw was one of Channel 9's star reporters. Just as Dana knew that Jeanine was being hailed as the wunderkind of the latest crop of female broadcasters.

Dana straightened in her chair, a rush of adrenaline pumping into her system. If there was one thing she relished, it was competition. The thrill of the hunt. Survival of the fittest.

The ballroom had grown hushed. All eyes turned toward Jeanine, then followed that woman's gaze to Dana. Low whispers proclaimed that both of them had been recognized.

"Six hundred," Dana proclaimed purposefully.

One of Jeanine's perfectly plucked eyebrows rose. "Six-fifty."

"Seven."

"Seven-fifty."

"Eight."

Jeanine's lips twitched a little at Dana's quick rejoinders, but her smile remained just as self-assured. "Eight-fifty," she said, using one finger to tuck a strand of hair behind her ear, a trademark gesture of sorts she used with every broadcast.

Dana was not impressed. In her opinion, Jeanine relied a little too much on her beauty-queen background to attract attention. Dana had been in the business long enough to realize that Jeanine's X-generation attractiveness might have its advantages, but she knew she had even more to offer. Jeanine might be younger, perkier, but Dana had elegance in her favor. That and experience and a "gut instinct" that had to be developed over the years.

"Eight-seventy-five."

"Nine hundred," Jeanine offered after a second's hesitation—and it was at that moment Dana knew she would win. Jeanine might offer a challenging smile. She might lounge in her chair and act completely cool and collected, but with that telling pause, Dana knew that—with a recent move and a new job—there was a limit to the other woman's pocketbook. A limit that was already within reach.

Deciding to force the issue, Dana drilled her competitor with an all-knowing stare. "Twelve hundred."

There was the tiniest of twitches from Jeanine's left eyelid. This time, her response was even slower in coming. "Thirteen-fifty."

When Jeanine nervously licked her lips, Dana instinctively knew she was at the edge. She'd probably bid more than she could afford. It was time to go in for the kill.

Slowly, deliberately, with an I-dare-you-to-take-me-on arch to her brow, Dana reached into her bag, withdrawing the ten crisp one-hundred-dollar bills that Dottie had bequeathed her. Then she flipped open her billfold to extract a Visa, a MasterCard and an American Express—all gold. Laying them on the table in plain sight, she glanced at Jeanine, making it clear to the woman that she had infinite resources at her fingertips.

"Fifteen hundred dollars," Dana said. She caught the auctioneer's eye to ensure she'd been heard, then looked back at Jeanine to guarantee the woman had understood her silent threat.

Dana would outbid her.

She *would* win.

"Ma'am?" the auctioneer prompted Jeanine.

For the first time that evening, the other reporter's smile faltered. She stared at the money, the credit cards, then at Dana. After several seconds, she caught the disc jockey's eager gaze and shook her head.

"Sold! To Ms. Dana Shaw of Channel 9," the emcee proclaimed a few moments later. "One thousand, five hundred dollars." She laughed, adding coyly in the microphone, "And the man isn't even here yet."

HE WAS LATE.

The battered pickup had barely come to a halt in front of the Red Lion Hotel before Sean O'Malley was reaching for the garment bag draped over the seat beside him.

"Thanks a lot, squirt." The parting shot was rife with layers of feeling—and he knew his sister Carol caught every one, because she grinned.

"You aren't still sore at Mary-Kate and me for signing you up for this bachelor auction, are you?"

"Yes."

She frowned, but the show of displeasure had little effect, since her eyes danced with evident merriment. "Come on, Sean," she wheedled. "It's for a good cause—and it isn't as if you haven't surrendered your dignity for charity before. You were Mr. January for the calendar, you know."

"Don't remind me," he said, checking the garment bag for the third time since leaving Logan. "I did it as a favor to help raise money, but even a year later, I'm accosted by strange women asking for my autograph."

"Poor baby," Carol soothed, but it was clear she found the whole situation highly amusing. "I'm sure that tonight will be different. You'll enjoy yourself."

"Like hell," he mumbled. "This is just your way of finding your older brother a date." She didn't deny it, and he felt pressed to add, "I've already had someone meaningful in my life, remember?"

"Liz has been gone for nearly a decade, Sean. Don't you think it's time to move on?" The words were gentle, nudging him in a direction he'd been reluctant to go for some time.

"I've been dating."

Carol sighed. "Amanda Campbell is nothing more than a friend—and you know it."

"So what's wrong with dating a friend?"

"Nothing. But we all know that particular relationship stalled long ago. Those of us at home want something more for you. Passion, adventure, romance."

"You've been reading those books again."

She chuckled. "No, brother, dear. We've been watching you raise eight siblings since Dad had his accident. It's time you had a family of your own."

"Ah. We're back to that familiar argument." Zipping the bag closed, he asked, "What makes you think that a woman who has to buy herself a date is going to give me those kids you think I should have, huh?"

"Maybe she will, maybe she won't. Either way, it's a start," she offered, revving the engine. "But Mary-Kate and I have already warned the others to be patient. We won't expect an engagement announcement for at least a month."

"Gee, thanks."

As he slammed the recalcitrant door closed, she threw him a cheeky wave.

"I'll be back with the truck by ten-thirty. Have fun!" he heard her say as she drove away.

Fun.

Fun?

He was about to be paraded in front of a ballroom full of women as if he were a prize bull at the county fair, and his sister thought he was going to have fun? Not likely. Not in the way she imagined. Sure, it was time for him to get back into the singles crowd again—he'd known that for some time. Just as he'd known Amanda wasn't right for him. Not for a lifetime. Not for midnight chats and mortgage payments and lying on blankets under the stars on hot summer evenings. No, he'd never been tempted in that direction. Not for a very long time. But somewhere, he knew there was a woman who would make him think twice about leading a solitary life. He just didn't think she would be here tonight, ready to plunk down her hard-earned cash for a chance to meet him.

Hooking a finger through a hanger, he tossed the garment bag over his shoulder and made his way to the side entrance of the hotel.

There were fewer guests here than there had been in front. Even so, those he saw wore a type of glittering New Year's Eve finery that was distinctly at odds with his own scuffed boots and faded jeans, the wool and fur of their coats much more upscale than the shearling jacket he preferred.

He didn't belong here. He was honest enough to admit that to himself. He was country born and country bred—and liked it that way. He didn't mind making a donation of his time to charity; as a volunteer fireman, he'd visited schools, taught CPR and helped the local Scout troop. He enjoyed such work, even though that would be the last thing he would admit to his sisters. But he didn't like drawing attention to himself, didn't like standing on stage, *didn't* like auctioning himself off like a side of beef. He was a simple man, preferring his relationships with women to be private.

Damn. He wished Carol and Mary-Kate hadn't done this to him—or if they'd insisted on such measures, he wished they hadn't left the terms of his agreement so vague. A week of entertainment. If asked, Sean would have offered an afternoon of horseback riding on the ranch, an old-fashioned sleigh ride—or a side of *real* beef, for hell's sake. Not seven days left open to some woman's vivid imagination.

He glanced at his watch, swearing again when he realized he was twenty minutes overdue, thanks to icy conditions in Sardine Canyon making anything but four-wheel-drive travel treacherous. The auction had probably started without him. Normally, that wouldn't have bothered him too much, but he'd been slated as one of the first bachelors to be sold. By being late, he would attract more attention than he'd bargained for.

Sighing, he prayed that this evening would end soon—and as painlessly as possible.

Sean was about to make his way inside when he was struck by an unusual sight. A woman stood just outside the exit, her back braced against the concrete wall, her coat open to the winter's breeze. She had just tamped down the antenna of a tiny cellular phone and was watching him—not in that curious, oh-my-gosh-is-it-really-him? kind of way, but more of a sensual appraisal.

Sensual?

He didn't know why that particular word popped into his head, but once it did, he found it difficult to banish. Especially when her eyes raked over his form from head to toe and her lips curved in the faintest of smiles.

"I wouldn't go in there if I were you."

Even her voice was unusual. Low, husky, whiskey smooth.

"Oh?" He wasn't sure why he responded, why he stopped just short of the door and acknowledged her. It definitely wasn't his style. Not when he was late for a prior commitment. Perhaps it was because she seemed vaguely familiar—as if he'd seen her somewhere before. Then again, maybe it was the way she made him feel as he towered over her. Tall, larger than life and distinctly masculine.

She bent one of her legs, propping the ball of her foot against the foundation, taking a sip of the bottle in her hand. Evian. Now, there was another phenomenon that Sean had never understood: paying a buck fifty for water that didn't taste half as good as the well water he had at home.

"It's a madhouse in there," the woman said after swallowing, her head moving in such a way that her chic, blunt-cut hair caressed the line of her jaw. It was hard to tell in the combined gloom of the night and the harsh glare of spotlights overhead what color the tresses were, but he was guessing a rich brown.

Maybe with a touch of red. Her eyes, though, were blue. A brilliant aquamarine blue.

Sean found himself taking a half step closer. "You wouldn't know if that bachelor auction has—?"

"Started?" She nodded, taking another swig of the cool water. "About twenty minutes ago."

He wished he could linger here and talk to this woman some more, but he knew he shouldn't. Such an action could be dangerous. Like playing with fire in the middle of an invitingly grassy field. One false move could leave him burned.

"Well...thanks for the information," he said when the silence stretched on too long, shimmering with its own brand of electric energy.

He'd taken less than two steps when she spoke again, "Like I said before, I wouldn't go in there."

Sean glanced over his shoulder to see her straightening with feline grace. It was then that her coat parted and he saw she was wearing some sort of russet-colored lace dress. The fabric was taut, stretchy, outlining a figure in perfect proportion—full breasts, narrow waist, sweetly flared hips. The garment was also short—very short—exposing a good deal of leg. Long, slender legs sheathed in silky hose with delicate feet shod in elegant suede pumps.

The jolt of awareness he felt just staring at her was stunning in its intensity. Stunning and completely unexpected. He hadn't felt this way in years. Not since he'd been a randy twenty-year-old farmhand trolling the Western dance halls for pretty girls.

Not since he and Liz had met, fallen in "lust" and decided to live together. A situation that had lasted less than three months.

"The women inside are out of control," she continued, dragging his thoughts away from the rapid thud of his heart. "If I were you, I'd steer clear of the whole lot. Frankly, I'm a little embarrassed to be a member of the same sex, what with all the whistling, whooping and stomping—it's like something out of a strip joint rather than a charity auction."

Sean damned the sensation when he felt a slight tinge of heat beginning to creep up his neck. He was normally very controlled, very reserved, but the thought of walking down a catwalk amid that sort of commotion was enough to make him balk.

Especially when he would rather stay here.

The thought hit him with the intensity of a punch to the stomach.

"Besides," the woman said, taking two steps toward him, coming so near he caught a whiff of her perfume, a hint of her warmth, "there's no reason for you to go inside, Sean."

Sean.

Sean.

The use of his name caused him to meet her gaze head-on. Those eyes. He'd never seen eyes so blue.

She smiled, a quick, gamine grin that created an answering reaction lower, so much lower, on his own anatomy.

"Hi, Sean." She held out a hand with long, beautifully manicured nails painted in red. A rich, autumn-leaf red. "I'm Dana Shaw. Your date."

The frigid winter air reverberated around them for some time before he could bring himself to say, "Excuse me?"

"The auction. I was the one who bought you."

"But I wasn't even—"

"There. I know that."

She reached to brush a stray piece of straw from his collar, the action incredibly intimate for a stranger, yet performed so smoothly, so easily, he wondered if she was even aware she'd touched him.

"The fact that you were the first bachelor on the program tended to rouse the audience to a fever pitch of excitement—especially once they were given a good look at the centerfold of you in that calendar. It was quite... revealing."

Again, he felt an inner heat creeping up his neck.

"Tell me, was that really perspiration? Or did they slather you with oil and spritz you?"

"Oil." He could barely manage to get the word out.

"I thought so." Again, she brushed at a speck of straw on his shoulder, making him wish his truck hadn't been so drafty, so dusty. "Anyway, the disc jockey leading the bidding had a wicked sense of humor. As soon as she saw the reaction from the crowd, she started talking about all of the experience you'd had with fires. The way that you could stoke a mound of hidden embers until licking tendrils of flame sprang free. She said that you knew just how to extinguish that flame, or how to control the heat so that it lasted long into the night. With all that going on, it didn't take much to bring the whole group to a frenzy of sorts—but I'm afraid it all came to a premature climax when I made my bid."

Sean felt the urge to clear his throat of the tightness that had gathered there. On the surface of things, the woman hadn't said a thing wrong, not a thing. But his heart had begun to thud as if she'd been deliberately provocative. Then again, maybe she *had* been deliberately provocative. Was that too much to believe?

"What was it about your bid that quieted them down?"

She offered him a smile worthy of the Cheshire cat, but didn't answer. Slipping her hand into her pocket, she withdrew a pen and a white card.

"I believe you volunteered for a week's worth of work."

"Yes." He wondered what she would have him do. Before arriving, he'd hoped that whoever "bought" him would demand he install smoke alarms and check her home for fire hazards. But such a scenario didn't fit this woman at all.

"Do you have any objections to beginning your duties the day after tomorrow?"

"The day after tomorrow?" he echoed in surprise, then shook his head. "No. That's fine. I can easily rearrange my schedule to accommodate that." In fact, if he were honest with himself, he would have to admit that for the first time since his sisters had broached the news of his involvement in the auction, he was feeling almost... well, agreeable.

"Do you have anything against elderly women, the smell of carnations or rumba music?"

He heard the words, saw them formed with her lips; nevertheless, they made no real sense to him. Sean nearly reached out to touch her himself, just to make sure this wasn't some sort of surreal out-of-body experience.

"No. I don't have a problem with anything like that."

"Are you allergic to dog hair, cigar smoke or Brylcreem?"

"No."

"Good." She scrawled something on the card and handed it to him. "Be there, day after tomorrow, noon sharp. Wear something comfortable and bring enough clothing to last you the full week."

Sean took the card, staring down at the Salt Lake City address she'd written. He was so puzzled at the curt summons and the lack of a clear explanation that she was halfway through the door before he stopped her.

"Hey! What's all this about, anyway?"

Again, that smile, that angelic, mischief-making smile.

"We're going to a birthday party," she announced sweetly. Then, with a waggle of her fingers, she was gone, melting into the crowd inside the hotel and leaving him to wonder about the significance of her inquisition.

And why he hadn't even questioned being told to bring a week's worth of clothing.

MUCH LATER, DANA HUMMED softly to herself as the elevator to her apartment building made its way to the top floor. After meeting with Sean O'Malley, she'd gone back to the auction to offer her support to Elise. Granted, she'd spent most of that time on the phone, arranging for a camera crew for the upcoming week, okaying the interview with Sean and scheduling advertising for her series. But she'd still been there to witness the way Elise had purchased her own bachelor.

The evening had been productive for both of them, Dana thought as she watched the bouncing ball of light trace her progress to the sixth floor. Knowing she had a limited amount of time to make arrangements for her upcoming visit to the Greycliff Retirement Village, Dana had excused herself from all but the first few minutes of the reception following the actual auction. She had lists to make, clothing to pack—a tuxedo to rent.

The ping of the elevator provided the perfect punctuation to her thoughts. As the doors slid wide, Dana sang under her breath, " 'Don't sit under the apple tree . . .' " while imagining her aunts' reactions as soon as they were introduced to Sean O'Malley.

They would be fascinated by him, she knew. He would immediately appeal to their sense of drama, their fanciful imaginations. Then, after Dana had proved she was more than capable of providing her own escorts, she could concentrate on her plans for an interview. One of those full-fledged, in-depth, make-them-squirm interviews that had made her famous in Utah. By the time she finished, the entire state would know why this calendar man had been so private all these months, so secretive.

So blasted attractive.

Slipping her key into the lock, she let herself into the dim foyer of her home, automatically punching the password into her alarm system, then reactivating it for the evening.

Sighing, she stretched, kicked off her shoes and reached to remove her earrings.

Yes. This would be the best birthday bash she'd been to yet. Such questions as "Why aren't you dating?" and "Why can't you find a nice young man to take care of you?" would be things of the past. Her aunts would stop sending her those awful blind dates. They would finally accept the fact that she was a grown woman. That she was capable of making her own decisions. That she wasn't doomed to spinsterhood because she'd chosen to remain single past the age of thirty.

"There you are, Dana."

The male voice appeared out of the silence, and Dana screamed, a hand flying to her throat.

From across the room, Fred Wallaby yelped, dropping a bag of potato chips onto the floor and causing the broken pieces to scatter.

Damn it! She'd meant to call to check if Fred was still here, but after she'd been interrupted...

"I didn't mean to scare you," he whispered, blinking at her with huge gray eyes behind glasses thicker than the bottoms of soda bottles. He shifted from foot to foot, obviously embarrassed. "But you locked me in."

Taking a deep breath to ease the pounding of her pulse, Dana closed her eyes and offered a silent prayer.

*Please, God. Please let Sean O'Malley cure my
aunts of their matchmaking, once and for all. I can't
take much more of this.*

I really can't.

Chapter Two

"Great sausage balls, Dana. Got any more?"

Dana bit her lip to keep from crying out in frustration as Thaddeus Wilcox shuffled into her living room, Fred Wallaby trailing closely behind the shorter man's heels. That morning, she'd literally found the pair on her doorstep when she'd returned from Channel 9. Thaddeus was the latest candidate in the long line of male companions her aunts had sent her way, while Fred...

Well, who knew why Fred had returned. After he'd been locked in her apartment for the better part of a day, Dana would have thought he'd steer clear of her.

Then again, she mused, shutting her suitcase and fastening the clasps, why shouldn't he be here? It wasn't the first time her aunts had mixed up their matchmaking arrangements and sent her more than one man at a time. The blind dates they arranged were becoming legendary in her small circle of acquaintances—each one more tenacious than the last, each one a living testament to the fact that there were still plenty of "nice" men, "good" men, "sweet" men, to be found in that mean, nasty, old world outside her window.

Thaddeus was no exception. A good four inches shorter than she—with the round face of a twelve-year-old and the hunched shoulders of a middle-aged man—he was a shy little thing who lived in a quaint bungalow with a garden and a parakeet named Bob. Or so he'd told Dana. At length. As he'd helped her heat up the sausage balls and Italian pasta soup left from the New Year's Eve lunch party as a brunch-time snack.

It didn't matter how many times Dana had tried to explain to these men that she wouldn't be home for the rest of the afternoon—wouldn't be home for days. Thaddeus had merely smiled at her and announced, "We'll stay here until you leave. We can't have you all alone with so much luggage to carry, now can we?"

Seeing him standing in her kitchen, expectantly waiting for an answer, she opened her mouth, irritated enough, frustrated enough, to send both of these men summarily packing. But when Thaddeus blinked at her, holding up the crystal dish, she didn't have the heart. She didn't have the *nerve*. Her aunts could be formidable opponents when crossed, and they would demand a debriefing as soon as she saw them.

Dana sighed, realizing that as far as her aunts were concerned, she often found herself reverting to an obedient adolescent. Dana supposed it was due to the fact that the three women had all but raised her after the death of her parents. She loved them to pieces. She would never do anything to hurt or disappoint them. But sometimes . . .

"Top shelf of the refrigerator," she mumbled in defeat, glad when the doorbell rang. She needed something else to think about. Something besides two sweet, well-meaning men lingering around her apartment because they didn't have anywhere else to go. Something besides the guilt she was experiencing because she couldn't wait to desert them in order to meet with Sean O'Malley. The man she'd paid to have as her escort.

The chimes rang again.

"Coming!" she shouted, hurrying into the foyer and wrenching open the door.

Her two favorite cameramen, Rick Bermen and Adam Westman, grinned at her from the hallway.

"Happy New Year!" Adam cried, holding up a bottle of his homemade rum punch. A half-dozen balloons had been tied to the top of the container and they bobbed crazily around his head.

Rick shoved a handful of plastic wineglasses in her direction and stepped into the tiny entryway. "Sorry we're a couple of days late in delivering the booze, but we went to a Christmas party."

"It just ended," Adam added. He peered into the living room, and Dana thanked her lucky stars that her two "dates" were nowhere to be seen.

"So you want us to follow you to Greycliff, huh?" Rick asked, seeing her luggage on the floor.

"Yes."

"Does O'Malley know you plan to interview him?"

"Not yet."

The two men exchanged glances.

"This could be dicey," Adam finally said. "Heather tried to get something on him last summer."

"Dixie a few months before that."

"Then there was Ellen around Easter..."

"Angela about Valentine's Day..."

"Fern soon after Civil Rights—"

"Stop it," Dana interrupted. "I know all about the past attempts, thank you very much. But this time—*this* time—he'll do a complete interview. Live. On Sunday afternoon."

"Uh-huh," Rick said, obviously unconvinced. Then he shrugged. "Frankly, I don't see why you'd bother. He's a local calendar man. So what?"

Her brow creased. "Yes, but there's a story there. I sense it. He's got a reason for being so reticent with the press, and I intend to find out why."

"Yes, but—" Adam abruptly stopped. "*Who is that?*" he whispered sotto voce, pulling her attention away from the mystique surrounding Sean O'Malley.

Thaddeus had just tiptoed past the dining room on his way back to the study, the bowl of sausage balls clutched in his hands, and Dana said dismally, "That's my latest date."

"The aunts again, hmm?" Rick remarked. "Which one sent him?"

"Mae."

"Figures. Why is he slinking into the study?"

She considered avoiding the question, but knew they'd discover the truth anyhow. "He and Fred are watching *The Glass-Bottom Boat.*"

"Fred?"

"June's choice."

Rick's brows rose. "Don't they know you're leaving town?"

Dana shrugged, "They didn't want me to carry my luggage down myself."

"Nice guys," Adam commented.

Nice. There was that word again. *Nice.* Dana was tired of "nice." Her aunts, never having understood why she'd always put her career first and all personal relationships last, were forever throwing "nice" men at her. Established men. Mama's boys and accountants and dentists and janitors. They wanted her to be wooed away from all talk of sound bites, Fresnel lights and word counts, and settle down. They didn't understand that Dana had never been interested in settling anywhere. She didn't cook—didn't want to learn. She hated to clean, couldn't stand ironing and absolutely gagged at such terms of endearment as "doodles" and "snookums."

"Why don't they just leave me alone?"

Dana didn't realize she'd spoken aloud until Adam answered. "Because your aunts don't think you're looking for a husband by yourself."

"I'm *not!*"

"And they don't approve of such an attitude. If you'd make an attempt—bring a date to those events they're always throwing—they'd probably stop sending you..."

"Beaver," Rick inserted. "That's who he looks like. That guy on 'Leave It to Beaver.' Except grown up."

"And out," Adam added under his breath.

Dana shot them a withering glance. "Bringing Sean O'Malley to Greycliff will change their minds."

"The only thing that will change their minds is a ring on your finger."

"And a wedding date."

Dana stared at the men, realizing they were right.

"If you could get O'Malley to play along to such extremes, it just might work."

"Greycliff..." Rick took a deep breath as if falling into a trance. "The whole area will be rife with atmosphere from the thirties and forties—Art Deco, big bands, dance floors gleaming with beeswax. It's a retirement community now, but it was once a hot-spot for intense romantic activity. Lovers meeting during a waltz. Clandestine trysts. Soldiers bidding fond farewells to their wives and sweethearts.''

He exhaled in a grand sigh, his gray eyes snapping. ''Then remember who will be there to meet you. April, Mae and June Flowers. Ex-U.S.O. beauties whose only goal in life is to see you married, settled and providing them with great-nieces and -nephews.''

The hazy dream world he'd been spinning began to vanish in a sick tide of reality.

Adam began to pick up the threads, ''They'll want you to mingle with their eccentric friends.''

''Play shuffleboard.''

''A round of bridge.''

''Dance the tango at their birthday ball.''

''Drink a little elderberry wine.''

''Take long walks on the terrace.''

''I hear they've been pressuring Mort the mortician to accompany you...''

''Oh, hell,'' Dana moaned, picturing the man Adam was describing—one of the orderlies who had taken a job at Greycliff because he was accustomed to living near his mother. He was forty-five if he was a day, with the bit of fluff at the tops of his ears his only claim to hair.

''That's it. You've convinced me. I'll get O'Malley to help me if it's the last thing I do. In the meantime, I need *your* help.''

Closing her eyes, she mentally pictured everything she would need to see her way through the next few days.

"Adam, get the equipment ready and be at Greycliff by tomorrow morning. Rick, see if Kathy in props on the third floor has some sort of cubic zirconium ring we can borrow. Surely they've used something of that sort for her 'Murder Theater' segment for PBS."

"Me! Aw, Dana, you know she's got some sort of thing for me," he groused.

"Which is why I'm sending you. You know how fanatical she is about loaning anything out."

He rolled his eyes.

"I want it big but tasteful—and make sure it glitters. Every time they look at me, my aunts need to be reassured that I'm about to be happily wed."

"And when that never happens?"

She offered them a mockingly pitiful groan. "Hopefully, my aunts will understand my pain when we call the whole thing off. Maybe they'll even give me a year or two to recover before sending the next round of mama's boys my way." She shooed at them, whipping open the front door. "Now, go!"

Rick jerked to attention, clicking his heels together and saluting. "Yes, ma'am!"

Adam merely grinned.

"And don't forget to pick up something in the way of engagement earrings or a necklace for me to wear to that blasted ball!" The two men were already rushing to the elevator, wrapping their scarves around their noses in preparation for the chilling weather they would have to brave. "It has to look like this man adores me, damn it, and nothing says that like diamonds!"

Rick waved to show he understood.

The ping of the instrument panel announced the arrival of the elevator car, and the doors slid wide.

The moment she saw him, a tall, gangly man dressed in a poorly fitting suit, sporting a dozen drooping carnations, Dana didn't need to hear him ask for directions to her own apartment. She knew he'd been sent here by her third aunt.

No.

No!

Slamming the door, she marched into the living room, startling the two men who were tiptoeing back to the kitchen, probably in search of another cheese ball.

"Let's go, gentleman. I need your help this afternoon. Tell me. Do either of you know where I can get a forties-style tuxedo?"

"YOU'RE SURE this is the place, Sean?"

Sean ignored the evident glee in Carol's voice, checked the card in his hand, then the numbers over the slender doorway on a building at least a hundred years old.

"That's what it says."

Carol couldn't quite muffle her snicker of delight. "It's an Arthur Murray School of Dance."

Sean fought the urge to swear aloud. "Maybe she works here."

"Uh-huh."

He glared at his little sister. "You're finding this all quite amusing, aren't you?"

She grinned even wider. "You told me that the woman planned to take you to a birthday party. But that party requires a weeks' worth of clothes, as well as some dancing lessons. It just gets better and better."

Sean wasn't so sure about that. If it weren't for the fact that he'd seen Dana Shaw, watched the way she'd moved, heard her voice, he knew he would be dreading this moment. But strangely enough, he wasn't. He was almost...anticipating their next meeting.

Without responding to his sister's teasing, he climbed from the truck, reaching into the bed for his duffel bag.

"Call me at my new apartment if you need a ride home," Carol said, revving the engine.

"Just remember that in a week, I'll be taking the truck back with me. You and your roommates had better have all your moving done before then."

"Sure, sure. Bye, Sean."

As the rattle and growl of the truck's engine faded into the distance, Sean slung the strap of his bag over his shoulder and tucked the tips of his fingers into the pockets of his jeans. Turning to stare up at the brick facade of the building in front of him, he almost—*almost*—considered calling a cab. But he didn't. Not even with the threat of dance lessons looming over his head.

Something had happened to him when he'd met Dana Shaw, something he couldn't quite explain. Their exchange had been so unexpected, so curious. Last night, cramped in a narrow cot in the living room of his sister's new apartment, he'd found himself thinking of Dana over and over again, wondering what twist of fate had caused her to bid on him. But more than that, he'd wondered what the next week would bring.

Spurred into action, he made his way up the cracked steps leading to the entrance of the dance school. The rough door squeaked, then sprang shut behind him, making a loud bang as he climbed up the cramped staircase. The speckled tile covering the treads had been worn away in the middle, marking the passage of countless pairs of shoes. The air around him resonated with the scent of leather, hair spray and perspiration.

Once at the top landing, Sean opened a second door with a frosted-glass inset containing a painted version of the school's logo. Stepping inside, he found a wooden floor the size of a basketball court spread out in front of him. Directly opposite, arched windows allowed the winter's weak light to make puddles of warmth on the shiny surface beneath his feet.

It only took a moment for his eyes to scan the rest of the area, to take in the mirrors on either side, the rows of folding chairs at one end, a barre along the other. But what caught and held his attention was the woman in the far corner.

Dana Shaw had red hair.

Red.

Closing the door soundlessly behind him, Sean took three steps into the room. Then stopped. Stared.

She was beautiful. Lithe, slim—nearly ethereal in the hazy light of the windows behind her. She was dressed simply—even scantily—in a pair of black tights, a running bra and a worn, ripped T-shirt knotted beneath her breasts. Judging by the patch of moisture at the front of her shirt and the damp tendrils escaping the twist of hair at her nape, she'd already had some sort of workout.

His eyebrows rose automatically when she stretched her arms overhead, linked her fingers, then bent at the waist, her face appearing upside down between her legs like a folded rag doll's.

As soon as she saw him, she started, snapping upright and whirling to face him, her hands automatically smoothing her hair. "You're here."

Her voice was breathless. Endearing.

"Yes," he replied needlessly, setting his duffel bag on the floor and propping one shoulder against the archway of the door. "I'm here."

She tugged at her shirt, but she needn't have bothered. The moment she left it alone, it rose to where it had been before, offering him a good deal of midriff.

"You're early."

"Is that a problem?"

"No." She smoothed her hands down her thighs. "But I'd planned to change."

"Not on my account, I hope."

She opened her mouth, hesitated, then closed it.

"So," Sean drawled, gesturing with one hand to the dance studio, "suppose you explain to me why you purchased my services, and why I'm here of all places."

She turned to make her way to her own gym bag, reaching inside to withdraw a bottle of water. Evian again. After twisting the cap, she drank long and deep, a droplet escaping her lips to wriggle its way down her cheek. Once she'd quenched her thirst, she sealed the container and put it back where it had been, hidden in her things.

Sean had the distinct impression that the whole routine had been a means to bide time, to think of a way to answer.

"You said something about a birthday party," he prompted when she didn't immediately speak.

"Yes, well..." She wiped a hand over her face. "I'm afraid there's a bit more to it than that."

"No kidding."

His wry response caused a smile to flash over her features. "You've got a sense of humor. Good."

Again, his eyebrows rose. "So why don't you explain why I'll be needing it?"

She planted her hands on her hips, studying him for the longest time. "Come with me."

When she began making her way to an office tucked into the corner over the stairwell, he followed her, liking the way her legs looked even longer, even more shapely, when covered in a light layer of spandex.

"These are my aunts," she said, pointing at some pictures on the walls. "The owner of this studio is an old friend of theirs and has included them in her wall of autographed photographs."

Yanking his thoughts back into line, he gazed up at the photographs lining one wall. The one she pointed to was a black-and-white publicity shot of three women on a makeshift stage surrounded by World War II infantrymen. Leaning closer, he took a better look. The three figures were identical—from the sausage rolls framing their faces, to the beaded, strapless costumes and open-toed shoes.

"Triplets?"

Dana nodded. "Yes. I guess the fact that there were three of them exactly alike was enough of a gimmick to help their careers. My aunts grew up in show business—you may have even heard of them. April, Mae and June Flowers?"

He regarded her in amazement. "You've got to be kidding. Who decided on those names?"

She shook her head. "My grandparents. They thought the springtime motif would be cute."

"What did your aunts think?"

Dana rolled her eyes by way of an answer, then continued with her story. "They were quite famous, actually. They even made a few films after the war ended."

"And now?"

She sighed, folding her arms. "Now they are turning seventy-five."

"So it's *their* party we'll be attending."

"Not just a party—a grand, five-day affair. All of the guests have been told to come dressed in costumes from the forties. There will be dance contests, big-band music, slide shows and a movie marathon. Then the whole thing will culminate with a full-fledged ball."

"Thus, the dancing lessons."

She nodded. "I don't suppose you can tango?"

"No."

"Rumba?"

"Sorry."

"Fox-trot?"

"I know the Texas two-step and the bear hug. Take your choice."

She sighed. "Thank goodness Maxine was able to fit in a private session."

"Maxine?"

"Your teacher."

He shook his head. "Sorry. I do the Texas two-step and the bear hug."

The look of dismay that spread over her features wasn't exactly what he'd expected.

"No. Oh, no. You've got to be proficient in the period steps. Otherwise, my aunts will never approve."

"Approve of what?"

"You. Me. *Us.*" Before he could ask for a clarification of that remark, she said, "I'll pay extra."

"I'm doing this for charity, remember."

"I'll send another five hundred dollars to Make a Wish."

Sean fought the astonished grin tugging at his lips and pretended to consider the idea. When she showed the first signs of a frown, he nodded. "Fine. I suppose in addition to the dancing, I'm to be an escort, as well?"

He was surprised when she didn't immediately respond. In fact, if he didn't know better, he'd say that a bit of a flush had entered her cheeks.

"Ye-es and no."

"Yes and no?"

"I do need you to serve as my escort."

"But..."

"But I need things to go a little farther than that."

"In what way?"

She eyed the photograph again, shaking her head. "My aunts are very eccentric and very, *very* possessive of me. I suppose they consider me the daughter they never had."

"I don't see the connection."

Dana used the tip of one fingernail to trace the exposed calf of one triplet. "From the moment they were born, my aunts have lived a life of glamour and adventure that most women would envy. But rather than being content with their lot, they have always regretted the fact that they never married. Therefore, when I began to show signs of following in their footsteps, of putting my career before any sort of personal involvement, they began a full-scale, strategic campaign to see me wed."

If the woman hadn't been so clearly distraught by it all, Sean would have laughed. "You can't be serious."

"Oh yes, I can," she responded fervently. "You should see the men who keep appearing on my doorstep—quite literally. *Nice* men with *nice* jobs and *nice* manners."

"How awful," he murmured in mock commiseration.

Her lips pursed when she detected the amusement he hadn't been able to banish from his tone. Without warning, she turned to face him, clasping the plackets of his jacket. "You have to help me. You have to pretend we're madly in love. That we're engaged to be married."

A chuckle escaped from his throat. He couldn't help it. She looked so earnest, so distressed. "Why should I do that?"

"It's the only way to stop them, the only way to keep wave upon wave of unmarried men from appearing at my door, from watching my videos and eating my sausage balls."

Her complete seriousness caused him to laugh openly now. She wasn't making any sense, none whatsoever, but he found he didn't mind. Not since she'd drawn herself close to him, lifting on tiptoe, her lips so near to his own that all he would have to do was bend a bit, put his arms around her waist and . . .

No.

Not yet.

But he was surprised by the way he was thinking in terms of future encounters of this variety. Staring down into her brilliant blue eyes, her hopeful expression, her moist, parted lips, he was reminded of the fact that he would be spending seven days with this woman. Seven whole days.

"Fine. I'll be your beau." Before she could move away, his arm swept around her waist, holding her against him. Her body was lithe and firm and fit nicely against his own. "After all, it's for a good cause."

She wilted against him in relief.

"But I think I should warn you first," he added softly, dipping to whisper into her ear, "I'm what my sister Mary-Kate calls a method actor."

"Oh?" Dana's voice was wispy, causing the muscles of his abdomen to tighten in response.

"Do you know what that means?"

She shook her head.

"It means that if I wish to convey an emotion, I need to experience it first."

Then he was closing the distance between them, touching her lips with his. Softly, quickly. Even so, the caress had the punch of a mule kick to his gut. She was so completely feminine, from the breasts that pressed briefly against his chest to the tickle of her hair.

When he drew back, he was pleased to see he wasn't the only one affected. Her mouth remained parted in disbelief at his boldness, her eyes widened even more.

Grinning, he touched her chin with his finger, gently closing her jaw.

"Don't worry, Dana," he murmured, liking the way she felt against him, the way her body had become sinuous and fluid in his embrace. "It shouldn't be all that difficult to convince three old women that we're in love. It might even be fun, don't you think?"

THREE HOURS LATER, Dana knew that her "fiancé" was beginning to regret his rash pronouncement. In that short period of time since he'd agreed to masquerade as her husband-to-be, Sean had been given a crash course of survival techniques for the upcoming week. Maxine had taught him a half-dozen dance steps. He'd been fitted with vintage clothing at a shop called Eclectic, and they'd rented a period tuxedo at the University of Utah Costume Shop. Then he'd been given a fresh haircut, manicure and a shave.

As they made their way into the underground garage of the Eagle's Gate apartment building, Sean stared down at his nails, frowning. "Was all this really necessary?"

"My aunts are sticklers for details." The sounds of their footsteps echoed against the bare concrete walls. "You'd better remember that. If we don't do everything by the book, they'll know this whole engagement is a fraud. You must be attentive, doting—give an impression of intimacy."

"I see."

The way he looked at her, long and hot and slow, made her believe that he would be more than capable of carrying off such a charade. Indeed, she found herself believing it a little herself. Enough that gooseflesh pebbled her skin and her heart skipped a beat.

Wrenching her own gaze away, she took a calming breath, inwardly chiding herself for half believing the glimmer of attraction she thought she found in his eyes.

It was all make-believe.

Just make-believe.

And she was a woman who dealt with cold, hard facts.

Dragging her brain back to the matter at hand, to the chill winter air, to the echoing parking garage and the fact that *she* was supposed to be the one in charge of this outing, she dug into the pocket of her coat.

"Here." She threw a jewelry box at him. "Open that up for me."

He released the catch as she fumbled in her bag for her car keys. Soon after leaving Arthur Murray's, the weather had turned foul. Rather than dealing with the congestion and parking problems associated with such conditions, they'd been using cabs to complete their errands. But the time had come for them to be on their way north to Greycliff.

Sean's soft whistle caused her to look up from the clutter of pens, dictation pads, makeup and hair-care essentials stuffed into her purse.

"*I* gave you this?"

She glanced at the engagement ring. Rick had done a wonderful job, choosing an emerald-cut "diamond" from the prop box. If not examined too closely, it could pass for a full-carat diamond.

"Yes. Why?"

"I must be doing better in the ranching business than I thought."

One of her eyebrows rose at that tidbit of information. "You own a ranch?"

A curiously guarded expression settled over his features. "Beef," he said succinctly, holding the ring out to her.

"Well, it isn't real, so don't worry." As an afterthought, she added, "Just don't tell anybody it's fake."

She slipped it onto the appropriate finger, then caught sight of her keys and fished them out of the sea of paraphernalia in her bag. "That's ours," she said, pointing to a low-slung roadster.

Sean gaped at the car, then at her. "This is yours?"

She shrugged. "It's my aunts', really. It's left in storage most of the year, but I've been ordered to drive it to the birthday bash."

Sean moved closer, running a caressing hand over the fender, the hood. For some reason, it caused a shiver to streak up her spine. His hands were strong, narrow, with long fingers and blunt-tipped nails. The manicure he'd been given had only highlighted their beauty, but not even the expensive grooming technique had been able to hide the calluses on his palms. Evidence of a man accustomed to hard work.

"What kind of car is it?"

She had to clear her throat in order to respond with any form of normalcy. "A 1942 Aston Martin, limited edition. It was given to my aunts when they signed their first movie deal."

He eyed her in concern. "It'll be a bear to drive if the roads get any icier."

She found it difficult to answer. He was still absently stroking the hood. Back and forth. Up and down.

"Dana?" he asked when she didn't respond.

Damn it, why couldn't she keep her mind where it belonged?

Inwardly cursing the way her normally organized mind had gone on some sort of vacation, Dana unlocked the door and slid in, leaning over to the passenger side to release the latch.

Sean dumped his bags and packages into the tiny space behind the seats, then gingerly folded his body into position. With his long legs, it was a difficult fit—and he looked far from comfortable. But he didn't complain. In fact, his attention seemed to have been diverted from her to the walnut dashboard and its controls.

For some reason, his distraction caused a burst of pique. Twisting the key, she brought the engine roaring to life, then with a squeal of rubber, she raced out of the parking lot and into the late-afternoon traffic.

She headed north, intent on Weber County nearly thirty miles away. Once there, she would follow the bench of the mountains to Ogden Canyon and head east another ten miles to the Greycliff Retirement Village.

They were nearing the mouth of the canyon—having made most of the journey in silence—when Dana knew she couldn't delay the inevitable any longer. As soon as they entered the narrow pass separating this section of the Wasatch Mountains, she would need all her attention on the road in order to navigate the hairpin twists and turns.

"We're almost there."

Sean looked at her then, his eyes a rich, dark blue. Intent. Incredible.

"Before we arrive, I think I should inform you of one or two additional things you'll need to know about my aunts."

"Oh?" The word was said with such care, she knew he'd sensed her hesitation.

"First of all, I should fill you in on Greycliff. It was once a very popular resort area—especially during the thirties and forties. They used to sponsor dances and picnics and excursions."

He watched expectantly.

"When my aunts retired from show business, they bought the place. By that time, it was empty and run-down. They refurbished it as best they could, but since they insisted on authenticity, some of the amenities are somewhat prone to failure. Remember that when you plan to use the hot water. My aunts have hired a handyman to take care of such problems, but he's run ragged most of the time—so be careful of having them volunteer you for duty."

"Okay."

Taking the first of the curves into the mountain pass and along the meandering path of the icy Ogden River, she said, "Now for some background on my aunts themselves. April is the oldest of the triplets—and she lords over them like a queen. I don't think she'll give you any trouble, but do not—I repeat, *do not*—let her involve you in a game of bridge."

"I don't play bridge."

"Good. Mae is the middle triplet. She has a few . . . quirks."

"Quirks." One of his dark eyebrows rose.

"Yes. She has a bit of a Greta Garbo complex."

"A what?"

"She imagines herself to be such a famous star that she must hide from society to keep from being hounded for autographs."

"I see."

It was clear he didn't, but as she rounded a curve and noted the lights of Greycliff shining through the falling snow, she knew she didn't have time to explain.

"June is the youngest of the three."

"Does she have any . . . problems I should know about?"

"Not really. But she's a sculptor, so don't be too surprised if she asks you to pose."

"What does she sculpt?"

"Nudes."

"Great."

"She also has a dog. Babbette. Please remember that its name is Babbette—no matter what else you might hear."

The roadster rattled over the old wooden bridge, and Sean leaned forward, peering out the windshield at the sprawling whitewashed building that awaited them.

Rolling to a stop, Dana killed the engine, then sat for a moment, her fingers clenched around the wheel.

Seeing the main door of the complex open a crack and a wizened face peer out, she knew there would be very little time now. The roadster had been recognized. Her aunts would be warned of her arrival.

"Let's go."

Climbing out of the car, she hiked her collar a little higher and squinted up at the thick, fluffy flakes. According to the weather service, the storm front wasn't supposed to hit until tomorrow. If this was the precursor to the main storm, what would the road conditions be like by the end of the week?

Shaking herself of such thoughts, she surged through the drifts to the main walkway. But when she would have brushed past him, Sean stopped her with a hand on her elbow.

"I don't know enough about you to carry this off. We really should have rehearsed some sort of story on the drive up here."

Dana caught her lower lip between her teeth, thinking. "It was love at first sight. We met two weeks ago and we're still learning about each other. That way, any inconsistencies could be explained."

"Where exactly did we meet?"

"At...my company business party. You were brought there by another woman, but the two of us hit it off."

"I didn't leave my date, did I?"

"Of course not. But you did ask for my number."

"Then what did we do?"

"Dinner, theater, dancing. The usual."

"For you, perhaps," he said.

"How so?"

"I don't really move in those sorts of circles. My life is much simpler. Much less harried." He took her left hand, moving it this way and that to study her ring. Even in the gloom, it sparkled with a life of its own. "I would have given you something different, I think. This is quite large for such delicate fingers."

The words had the power to cause her skin to tingle and an effervescent heat to move into her chest.

"Maybe something with color to offset the diamond. Sapphires or rubies."

She loved rubies.

"When did we become engaged?" he asked.

"Last night. That way, they won't be suspicious that I didn't call."

"Did I kiss you?"

"What?" She had to pull her mind back to what was being said.

"When I gave you the ring, did I kiss you?"

"Oh. Well, uh, of course."

"Did you enjoy it?"

She cleared her throat to relieve it of its sudden tightness. The brief embrace they'd shared in the dance-studio office rushed into her head. "Yes."

"Are you certain?"

"Mm-hmm."

"Let's make sure."

Then he was pulling her near with a gentle tug of her hand. His head dipped toward her, a finger tipping her chin.

Good. He tasted as good as she'd remembered. Clean, warm and vibrantly male. It had been so long since she'd been kissed like this. Not tentatively, not hesitantly, but willingly, forcefully, by a man who was no stranger to such embraces.

His lips were amazingly warm considering the weather and the less than adequate heater in the roadster. Even with her eyes closed, she could feel his hand at her hip, burrowing beneath the hem of her parka, burning through the wool of her sweater.

A knot was forming in her stomach, one she recognized as excitement and the first hint of arousal— and the fact astounded her. She had not gone through her life without feeling passion, but never had she experienced it so quickly before. With a man who was little more than a stranger.

When he backed away, Dana discovered she was breathless. She blinked up at him, liking the way his eyes smoldered. The pupils were large, the irises darkening to a blue-black that was hypnotic.

"There. That looks a little better."

"What?" She could barely force the word out.

"You look more...mussed."

"Oh." It was an effort to talk. She kept wondering what it would feel like if she wriggled her own fingers beneath his jacket to the hard muscles beneath.

Somewhere from the corner of her eye, she saw the front door being flung open. Sean must have seen it, as well, because he said, "Somehow, I think your aunts would approve of such attention to detail."

"Yes."

His smile was rich, warm, filled with secrets. To Dana, a woman who made her living from uncovering such mysteries, such a response was nearly as heady as his kisses had been.

"Come on. It's time for the performance to begin."

Then he was leading her forward to where April, Mae and June Flowers were looking on with curious eyes.

Chapter Three

Sean slipped his hand a little more tightly around Dana's waist, liking the way her hip bumped intimately with his own. He hardly looked at the elderly women watching their progress, concentrating instead on the way Dana fit so easily against his side, her strides matching his.

"Hello!" Dana called out to her aunts. "I'd like you to meet Sean." She held the hand out with the ring and added, "My fiancé! We became engaged just last night!"

Sean braced himself for a barrage of questions, anticipating the way his own family would have reacted to such an announcement. But the squeals of joy never came. There were no rapid-fire questions being directed at them with no time for a logical answer. There was just a silence. An overwhelming, disbelieving silence.

Bending, Sean was about to ask Dana if this was a normal reaction for such an important piece of news, but at that moment, the door behind her aunts opened even wider and two men sporting heavy cameras on their shoulders swung their lenses in Sean's direction.

He froze. Cameras? *Cameras?*

His abrupt movement threw Dana off stride, but she automatically corrected the slight stumble and assumed her best posture, as well as a quick smile.

A smile he recognized as the same one that often flashed at him from the depths of his television set.

Damn.

Damn, damn, *damn.*

Now he realized why Dana had seemed so familiar to him that first evening. She was one of the anchorwomen for the Channel 9 news team. Granted, Sean rarely had the time for watching television. When he did, he invariably scanned the channels for sports and the weather—but he still should have recognized her immediately. He should have recognized her name.

"Damn."

This time, the curse escaped in a barely audible growl. Unfortunately—or perhaps fortunately—it was loud enough for Dana to hear.

She paused, glancing at him over her shoulder. The overt expression of joy she'd adopted for her aunts wavered when they made eye contact.

"What's wrong?" she asked under her breath.

Realizing that they had an audience—not just her aunts, but the whole world, for all he knew, he grasped her hand tightly in his and brought it to his lips, pretending to kiss the ring as a show of affection. It took all the will he possessed to keep from grinding her fingers together.

"What the hell is going on here, Ms. Shaw?" he growled.

He had to give her credit for her show of genuine confusion.

"I don't know what you mean. I told you about my aunts."

"Aunts, hell. I'm talking about the camera crew."

Her lips formed a silent "Oh."

"What are they doing here?"

She stepped closer, swinging her arm around his neck and offering him a hug. "Let's not talk about it now."

His own arm snapped around her waist, crushing her close. Even with his anger, his body absorbed the contact with a jolt of adrenaline.

"I think we'd better talk, Ms. Shaw."

"This really isn't the time or the place."

"*Now*, Dana," he insisted next to her ear. Flicking a glance at the group on the porch, he hoped that he and Dana gave the impression of two crazy-in-love people who couldn't manage to keep their hands off one another.

"I'm a reporter."

"No kidding."

"On Channel 9."

"I already figured that out, Ms. Shaw. What I don't know is why there are two cameras pointed our way."

"It's part of a feature segment I'm doing. 'Creative Dating in the Nineties.'"

He swore again, and she started, then kissed his cheek.

"Let's talk about this later," she said, disengaging herself and pulling him resolutely to the entrance of Greycliff Village.

Sean plastered a wide smile on his face. Not for Dana. Not for her aunts. But for the benefit of the cameras. He prayed he didn't look like a total fool, prayed that the news of his "engagement" wouldn't be one of the headlines on the ten-o'clock news. He vowed to have a talk with his sisters as soon as he returned home. This was absolutely the last time he participated in one of their harebrained matchmaking schemes.

With each step closer to the cameramen, his dread increased, memories washing over him like a bitter tide. He'd already suffered through one media-instigated circus when his photograph in the calendar had been released. He'd endured the women who had followed him in their cars, or called dispatch to arrange "personal fire drills." One woman had even had the audacity to steal his dry cleaning in order to meet him. He didn't want that sort of attention. Not now. Not when he was due for another review by the state social services as an appropriate guardian for his three youngest sisters.

His grip on Dana's hand tightened, conveying his anger. But she wasn't paying attention to him. She had focused all her energies on the three elderly ladies who waited on the porch.

Sean's eyes narrowed as he took in the trio of wizened women with their pastel-colored hair. This was what had caused Dana Shaw to develop such an elaborate charade? *This?* The little old ladies didn't look as if they could harm a fly, let alone instill the kind of worry Dana had displayed the past few hours.

"Sean, these are my aunts," Dana said as she and Sean came to a halt on the top step.

Even in their advanced age, the triplets were nearly identical. But certain mannerisms and a wealth of living had given their faces different lines and creases, so that Sean was able to tell them apart.

A woman with her hair rinsed a pale blue stepped forward, a thin cigarillo hanging from her lower lip, her body covered in a Nixon-administration-aged shirt dress in an indiscriminate color of beige.

"This is April."

The woman blinked at him through thick glasses that caused her eyes to be magnified three times their normal size. When Sean politely extended his hand, she gripped it with the strength of a wrestler.

"Do you play bridge?" she rasped with the scratchy, baritone drawl of a lifelong chain-smoker.

"No, ma'am."

"Canasta?"

"No, ma'am."

"Poker?"

His hesitation was answer enough, and she grinned, taking the cigarillo from her mouth and brandishing it wide with Bette Davis-like flourish. "I'll talk to you later," she said coyly before the next triplet crowded forward.

"This is June."

"So pleased to meet you."

She looked like a giant Easter egg with her lavender hair and jewel-toned caftan. She took his hand with both of hers, then wouldn't release it. Instead, she began to rub his wrist, his forearm.

"Such a strong form. You must lift weights."

Sean shot a glance in the direction of the cameras and fought the urge to bolt.

"Tell me," she purred, "have you had your bust done?"

Dana quickly stepped between them, gripping Sean's shirt at the waist—a little more tightly than was necessary.

"Aunt Mae? Wouldn't you like to meet Sean?"

The last triplet had stayed a few feet away from the group. In fact, her attention seemed to be centered on the cameras. She was leaning ever so slightly against the porch railing, her chin tilted up, a pair of ridiculously large sunglasses perched on the end of her nose.

"Aunt Mae?" Dana prompted when the woman didn't respond.

As soon as the cameras swung her way, Mae straightened with a lithesome grace, cocked her head ever so slightly to one side and offered a guileless, indulgent smile. Of the three sisters, she was the only one who'd seen fit to "dress" for the occasion—and Sean couldn't help thinking she looked like a retirement-aged Ginger not yet rescued from "Gilligan's Island." Her beaded gown was incredibly formal, as was her mink stole, but she carried them off with aplomb.

Pouting in the direction of the cameras and flipping a lock of pale pink hair away from her forehead, she reached for her glasses and slid them free with tantalizing reluctance. Holding the other hand up in front of her face, as if wishing to shield herself from the prying eyes of a thousand fans, she finally turned in Sean's direction.

A hushed stillness settled over the covered portico. The winter air seemed to grow tense and expectant. Even the other sisters had grown still, tamping down their evident suspicion as they waited for Mae's reaction.

In Sean's opinion, the whole exchange had been odd. After all, if these women were accustomed to throwing men Dana's way, he'd expected at least some sort of excitement when introduced to Dana's fiancé. But even as he prepared himself for such a thing, as he waited for Mae to offer some sort of gracious how-do-you-do, he watched the color drain from her face.

Her expression grew stricken, and she braced herself against the railing whispering, "Ramone?"

The air became suddenly brittle. Hushed. Expectant.

"Ramone?" she said again, the word emerging as a plaintive whisper.

Then she dropped her arms to her sides and sobbed, "Ramone, why have you done this to me?"

Sean looked to Dana, stunned, but she seemed just as startled as Mae dashed inside.

June was staring at him now, her own lip trembling. "Oh, oh, oh," she whispered. "You shouldn't have upset her that way. You really shouldn't." Then, pressing her fingertips to her mouth, she whirled and left.

Only April remained, her lips pursed. Throwing the butt of her cigarillo to the ground, she stomped on it, then marched to Sean. "You bastard," she growled. "Can't you see what you've done?"

Before Sean knew what she intended to do, she drew back her hand and slapped him full across the cheek.

"That will teach *you* a lesson, mister," she snapped before whirling and storming inside.

It was the slam of the door that roused Dana from her astonishment. "What was all that about?" she whispered.

Tearing her gaze away from the still-shuddering portal, she met Sean's glare, Rick's openmouthed stare and Adam's none-too-subtle snickering.

"Do you want us to keep filming?" Adam asked.

"No. No!"

Not until the two men had lowered their equipment from their shoulders did she speak again.

"I apologize, Sean. I don't know what got into them."

Judging by his stony glare, he didn't believe her. He didn't believe her at all.

"Guys, can you excuse us?" she said in Rick and Adam's general direction.

From the corner of her eye, she saw them shrug and disappear indoors. But most of her attention was focused on Sean, on the way the imprint of her aunt's hand still glared red from his cheek.

"I'm so sorry." She reached to touch it, but his fingers snapped around her wrist, holding her away.

"What the hell just happened here?"

She could only shrug. The tight, masculine band holding her still was having an odd effect on her pulse, causing her heart to thump more insistently than it should.

"I don't know. I thought they'd be ecstatic that I brought a *fiancé* to their party. I never imagined that they would . . . that they . . ."

Wriggling her hand, she managed to free it. Using just her fingertips, she explored the bright mark on his cheek.

"Does it hurt?"

A muscle twitched at his jaw.

"What kind of game are you playing, Ms. Shaw?"

Ms. Shaw. Not Dana.

Her stomach made a sad sort of flip-flop. He was angry—really angry. And after the scene her aunts had just made, she couldn't blame him. But what made things even worse was that it was clear that Sean thought she had expected the triplets to behave this way. That fact, combined with the surprise arrival of the television cameras, had doubly damned her in his eyes.

"I honestly don't know what just happened here."

He didn't believe her. She knew he didn't believe her. But he took a step back—and for the first time, Dana realized she'd been holding her breath.

"Then I suppose you'd better find out."

It was a dismissal. A blatant command. One that Dana could not refuse.

"Yes," she said weakly, backing away. When her shoulder brushed the lintel, she asked, "What will you do in the meantime?"

He regarded the falling snow. The wind had begun to intensify, causing it to swirl in a hypnotic fashion.

"I think I'll wait right here."

"But the..." she began to protest, ready to cite the cold, the weather, the inhospitable surroundings. But she supposed his arrival at Greycliff had been even less welcoming than the show Mother Nature was providing.

"I'll be back as soon as I can."

"Fine."

Still hesitant to leave him, she offered, "You could bring our things in from the roadster."

The way he glared at her proclaimed clearly enough that he would like nothing better than to climb into the car and make his way back to Salt Lake City.

Afraid that if she said another word, he might be tempted to do just that, Dana darted into the reception room of Greycliff Village. Ignoring Adam and Rick, who were standing by the coffee machine mere feet away, she ran in the direction of the elevator, which would take her to her aunts' suite of apartments on the third floor.

Rick grinned, taking a sip of the bitter brew in his foam cup. "How do you think things are going, Adam?"

Adam blew on ink black liquid in his own cup. "Splendid, wouldn't you say?"

"Splendid," Rick agreed readily.

"I don't suppose we'll be needed for an hour or two."

"I wouldn't anticipate it."

"'Oprah,' Mr. Westman?"

"Naw," Adam replied, folding his length into an overstuffed chair and reaching for the remote attached to a low table with a plastic cord. "The village has cable, Mr. Bermen. Let's find a station with wrestling."

"Ooh. Good idea, Mr. Westman."

"AUNT MAE?"

Dana rapped her knuckle on the door, resting her ear to the panels in an effort to hear what was happening inside.

"Aunt Mae, what's wrong?"

There was no answer, no noise—not even a sniffle to reassure Dana that her aunt was even inside.

"Drat," Dana muttered to herself, reverting to the age-old habit of tempering her language whenever she was near her aunts. Indeed, whenever she was with them, she often felt as if she regressed, becoming a child again. A child who minded her p's and q's and did her best to please.

After another thump of her knuckle, she surrendered to the inevitable, moving across the hall to Aunt June's door.

"Aunt June?" She knocked, she rang the bell, she waited. Still no answer. "Blast and bother."

"Come now, Dana. As a reporter, you can do better than that."

She jumped when Aunt April spoke directly behind her. Spinning, she frowned as April took a cigarette case from her pocket and withdrew a golden lighter.

"Those things are bad for you," Dana said out of habit.

"So sue me." April chose a nasty-looking colored cigarillo and lit it, filling the hall with its pungent aroma.

"Isn't this a no-smoking area?" Dana asked wearily, leaning against the wall.

April shrugged. "I don't see any signs."

The fact that a potted palm had been dragged strategically in front of the announcement wasn't lost on Dana, but she didn't bother to argue. No matter the confrontation, if it involved Dana and her aunts, she never won. Never.

Dana sighed, demanding, "What's going on here, Aunt April?"

April squinted at her through the smoke, the glasses she wore making her eyes seem that much more penetrating.

"You don't know. You really don't know?" she asked.

"Know what?"

April gestured with her cigarillo. "That man down there."

"My fiancé?"

"Whatever... He's all wrong for you."

"How can you possibly know that? You haven't even met him properly."

"We *know* him, the cad. He hasn't changed."

Dana huffed in frustration. "What are you talking about?"

"Ramone." She said the word as if it left a bad taste on her tongue.

"Who is Ramone?"

"Ramone C. Peruga, a Cuban band leader."

"Sean is not—"

April continued without pause, "He swore he loved me, swore to marry me—but little did I know he was offering the same avowals of undying love to Mae and to June."

Dana still wasn't sure what her aunt was trying to say. "You mean that the three of you think Sean is this Ramone...Pergula person."

"Peruga. *Peruga!*" The name rolled from April's tongue with a distinctly Hispanic accent.

"But that's nonsense. The man you're talking about would have to be at least eighty-five years old."

April's lips tightened.

"That is *not* Ramone C...."

"Peruga."

Dana's fingers drummed against the wall behind her. She knew it was a nervous, telling reaction, but she couldn't help it. Of the triplets, April was usually the sensible one. The logical one.

She grabbed the cigarillo from her aunt's hand and sniffed it carefully.

"What are you doing?" April demanded.

"Just checking," Dana said. "Making sure you haven't been into some funny sort of tobacco."

April snatched the cigarillo back. "Even if I had been, you wouldn't be able to do anything about it, missy."

True enough.

"Aunt April," Dana began again, trying to adopt a reasonable tone. "Surely you don't think that Sean and Ramone C. Pelu—"

"Peruga."

"Peruga . . . are the same person?"

April blinked behind the magnified lenses. "I didn't say that *I* did."

Aha. Now they were getting somewhere.

"June doesn't think he is, either, does she?"

April took a deep drag.

"She doesn't, does—?"

"No, she doesn't," April admitted quickly, rebelliously.

"Then it's just Mae who's the problem."

April jabbed the cigarillo like an accusing finger. "I don't like him."

"Who? Ramone or Sean."

"Either."

"But you don't even know Sean. He's a nice man. Once you get to know him, you'll love him like I do." The words tasted sour on her own tongue.

"How can I like a man you're ashamed of?"

"Ashamed?" Dana echoed.

"You didn't call to tell us about him. You didn't even bother to warn us. You just appeared here, with that gaudy ring on your finger, that . . . that *man* hanging on your arm."

Dana closed her eyes, rubbing at the spot between her eyebrows where her head was beginning to ache.

"You're right, Aunt April. I should have phoned you. I should have told you about him the night we met." She hated lying. It was so mean, so low, so damning. "I just thought I'd surprise the three of you."

April was piercing her with a stare that could have melted glass. "You succeeded quite admirably."

Dana shifted guiltily from foot to foot, feeling like a child who'd been caught stealing.

"Your aunt Mae isn't . . . well, you know."

As a matter of fact, Aunt Mae did have a heart murmur—something she'd had since the age of seventeen. Her main problem, however, was that she was a trifle batty, but no one would dare admit such a thing out loud. Not even Dana.

"It might not be a reasonable reaction, but she thinks that man is Ramone C. Peruga."

"Yes, ma'am," Dana whispered guiltily.

"It's going to take some explaining to convince her otherwise."

"I know."

"And her heart . . ."

Dana was feeling more and more wormlike.

". . . it isn't as strong as it could be. The shock won't help her any. You're going to have to do something to convince her that Ramone hasn't risen from the dead."

Finally, a ray of hope. A way to make amends.

She drew back her shoulders, touching her aunt's arm. "You've got to help me. Please. Let's have dinner together. That way, Mae can get to know him—you all can. See that he's a nice man."

There was that word again. *Nice.* But in Sean's case, it seemed far too tame, far too inadequate.

Aunt April's lips pursed, and she took a drag on her cigarillo. By that slight hesitation, Dana knew she'd been given a reprieve.

"Please," she added softly.

"I'll talk to the girls," April finally agreed. "I'll even try to talk some sense into Mae. We'll have a little something at my place like we'd originally planned. I'll give you twenty minutes to fetch the rounder. Not a minute more."

Dana felt her muscles in her shoulders relaxing one by one. "Thank you, Aunt April."

But as she turned and made her way to the elevators, she could only pray that Sean would prove cooperative, as well. For all she knew, he might back out of the whole deal.

Frankly, she wouldn't blame him if he did.

DANA STEPPED onto the portico, closing the front door behind her. Wrapping her arms close around her waist, she stared at the man still waiting for her report.

She'd hoped that the noise of the storm would cover her arrival, that she would have an element of surprise in her favor when she confronted him again, but such a wish wasn't about to be granted.

"My aunts would like to have you join them for dinner."

The temperature on the porch was arctic. The wind had increased to near-gale-force, and the snow was swirling around them with a stinging intensity. All of that, however, seemed downright tropical compared to the stare that Sean shot her way.

"They would, huh?"

Even in the relative shelter beneath the eaves, snow crusted his dark hair and had begun to collect on his shoulders. Nevertheless, he was slouched in one of the Adirondack chairs as if he were trying to get a tan.

"It will be a small affair. Only family."

"I see."

"They won't require you to dress." When one of his eyebrows rose, she added quickly, "Dress up. For dinner."

"That's very kind of them." But he didn't sound pleased. Didn't even sound placated. "Tell me, will I be needing protective padding?"

Dana felt a flush climbing up her cheeks.

"I'm sorry about that." She tugged another chair close to him and sat gingerly on the edge, hugging her coat over her knees. "It seems that you bear a striking resemblance to a man from their past."

"Oh, goody." There was no disguising his sarcasm.

"As far as I've been able to gather, the three of them were involved with a Cuban band leader named

Ramone C.... something or other. Aunt Mae thinks that you are that man."

"That isn't possible."

"I know that. I think April and June will help her to see reason."

"They didn't seem any less fanatical about the issue than your aunt Mae."

"I think their reactions stemmed from their concern for Mae. She isn't entirely well. April and June are very protective of her."

He made no comment.

"Once they get to know you, I'm sure they'll be sweet and adorable...." Her words trailed away.

"But..." he prompted when she hesitated.

"But it would really help if you could do your best during dinner to convince them that you *are* my fiancé. That you love me deeply, passionately, adoringly. That way, they will look past the surface similarities to you and that Cuban gigolo."

The moment the words were out, she wished she could retract them. After all, wasn't she paying Sean to escort her in a manner of speaking?

He took a deep breath. "I'm beginning to believe you got a bargain when you bid on me at the auction."

"I'll send another one thousand dollars to Make a Wish," she offered hopefully, knowing that what she was requiring this man to do over the next week was far beyond the intentions of the auction organizers.

The air rushed from Sean's lungs. "Fine. But no cameras."

"I—"

"*No* cameras," he repeated firmly. "This little get-together is off-limits to the rest of the world."

She quickly agreed, not bothering to inform him that she wouldn't dream of having the next few hours available to the public. It would be far too galling.

"Very well."

He held out his hand. "Shake on it."

She allowed his fingers to close over her own, intending the gesture to be purely businesslike. But as soon as their skin met, melded, she shivered.

And not from the cold.

Chapter Four

Dana rose from her chair, still holding his hand, and tugged Sean upright, drawing him into the foyer. The blast of warmth caused her skin to tingle alarmingly.

"Where's this supper supposed to be held?"

"Aunt April's apartment."

"The smoker?"

"Yes."

As they made their way through the waiting area, Rick and Adam rose, automatically reaching for the paraphernalia at their feet.

"Relax, guys," she said. "You're done for the night. Check with the front office about where they've arranged for you to sleep."

"Right-oh," Rick said, stretching. "By the way, did you hear about the roads?"

Dana paused, a sinking sensation settling into her stomach. "No. What?"

"They've closed Weber and Ogden canyons due to ice and high winds."

She felt Sean's grip tighten.

"For how long?"

"Until the storm clears," Adam offered. "Which—according to the National Weather Service—could be days."

"Maybe a week," Rick added.

Dana groaned. "That means we'll be stuck inside, hour after hour, with my aunts."

Sean swore.

The two men began to gather their things.

"But don't let it worry you," Adam said with a smirk.

"Just have yourselves a grand time with the girls," Rick joined in.

Then they laughed, heading in the direction of the front office.

Dana waited for some time, expecting Sean to say something. When he didn't, she dared to sneak a peek at his face.

It was resigned.

Hard.

Intriguing.

"Well. It appears as if my fate is sealed. Like it or not, I'm here for the duration with you and your kooky aunts."

"Yes," she supplied hesitantly.

"Then let's get this evening over as soon as possible."

They made their way to the elevator in an uncomfortable silence. Through it all, Sean clenched his jaw, wondering how he'd managed to fall into a position where one old woman thought he was some reincarnated Cuban band leader and two more believed him to be a masher. The only way to convince them he wasn't either one was to feign an infatuation for Dana Shaw. *How in the world did such an apparently sane woman end up with such bizarre relatives?* he wondered.

They stepped into the elevator car, and Dana pushed the button for the third floor.

"Are you sure you don't want to change into some dry clothes first?"

He didn't even consider the idea. "No."

"You could take off your coat."

"In a minute."

That was the bulk of their conversation. Short, brief, blunt—the gist of the words should have been enough to stoke Sean's anger for hours.

But it wasn't.

As the seconds ticked by and the aging, rickety elevator with its curlicue-gilded doors inched its way upwards, Sean found himself riveted by the woman at his side. She looked so earnest, so apologetic, so...

Vulnerable.

These old ladies had her rattled, Sean realized suddenly. Each night, the world saw Dana Shaw as a woman in control, one who was totally calm, collected and at ease with any situation. Even Sean had been confronted with that persona so many times, he had accepted it without question.

But he was being given a glimpse into the very heart of her. He was seeing a woman who cared so deeply about her aunts that she would turn her own world upside down to give them happiness.

Without really thinking about the consequences of his actions, Sean reached out, pushing the Stop button. The ancient elevator ground to a halt, then jiggled unsteadily as if it weren't sure what had happened.

"Hey!"

Dana turned wide, accusing eyes his way, and he had to fight the urge to grin.

"What was that for?" She released her grip on his wrist to fold her arms beneath her breasts—and he wondered if she knew how such an action caused them to plump and press against the soft wool of her sweater.

"I need some answers," he said, stepping closer, crowding her against the wall. "This time, I'm not walking into the lion's den unprotected."

She licked her lips, her gaze darting nervously, scanning the cramped space and settling everywhere but on him.

"I've told you everything I know. Ramone C. Peruga was a Cuban band leader hired by the U.S.O. He must have been some sort of Don Juan because he romanced my aunts, promised to marry each one, then deserted them all. Evidently, Mae took the rejection the hardest.''

He made her nervous. Sean knew he did. Very nervous. It was there in the way she glanced longingly at the control panel, the way she shifted from foot to foot. The fact was enough to tug even harder at the corners of his lips, but he couldn't let her see it. Not yet.

Sean placed his hands on either side of her waist, gripping the brass railing. Schooling his features into a frown, he said, "That's not what I mean. The fact that your aunts have taken a dislike to me because I bear some faint resemblance to a former boyfriend is beginning to seem more and more logical to me.''

He closed the remaining space so that less than a handbreadth of tension-fraught air separated them. "No, what I need to know is why these women have such a hold on you.''

She laughed, tossing her head.

It was a mistake, and they both knew it. He didn't believe the show of humor was genuine, and the action merely offered him a better view of the creamy flesh of her neck.

"Tell me," he murmured, bending lower, entranced by her wide eyes and velvety skin, "why do their opinions mean so much to you?''

She took a breath, a shuddering, uneven breath that caused her breasts to come into contact with the leather of his coat. He wished now that he'd responded to her offer of removing the garment.

Somehow, in the space of a heartbeat, the actual conversation had become secondary. In its place came a need, a wish, a hunger. A desire to see if the sensations they'd encountered during their previous brief embraces had been real or merely a figment of their imaginations.

"My aunts . . ." She fell into silence. A taut, pregnant silence.

"Yes."

"My aunts raised me when I . . ."

He was watching her lips, noting the way they formed the words even though he didn't really hear them, didn't really care what she said as long as she kept talking.

She must have experienced a similar reaction because her hands lifted to spread wide over his chest.

"Yes . . ."

"They raised me when my own parents were killed in a hotel fire."

"How awful."

She shrugged, and somehow the action brought her even closer, so that their hips brushed. "I was only three at the time."

"Were they good to you?"

Her hands curled around his lapels. "Yes. Oh, yes. My aunts were the best parents anyone could ever hope to have."

"Even though their mannerisms were . . ."

"Odd," she supplied, on tiptoe now, her lips hovering just below his. "It sometimes made bringing friends home or parent-teacher conferences a little trying."

"But you adopted a sort of love-me-love-my-aunts attitude."

"Yes."

It was a mere sigh against his lips.

"And now that you're grown, whenever you're with them..."

"I feel like a kid again," she admitted, the words so close, he could feel them on his lips. "I don't want to hurt them, I love them dearly, but I'm thirty years old, damn it...."

Then all explanations and all thought ceased as their mouths met, clung, shifted. A white-hot flare of passion burst between them, making the elevator seem that much smaller, their cocoon of solitude that much more intimate.

Sean slid his arms around Dana's waist, taking her weight, drawing her upward against him so that they were crushed together, man to woman, chest to chest, heart to heart. He could feel her hunger and more, a sinuous energy that he had never experienced in any other woman. One that made her his equal—and indeed, an aggressor of sorts. For each caress, she countered with one of her own; for each advance, she offered another.

He felt her strip his coat from his shoulders and her legs twine eagerly between his. Not to be outdone, he slid the loose shawl collar of her sweater low, exposing a creamy shoulder and the black silken strap of her bra. That scrap of underwear was his undoing. Bending, he kissed the hollow he'd exposed, suckled, nipped.

She became a wild thing in his arms, her back arching to allow him better access to the spot he'd found.

"We shouldn't be doing this," she whispered, her voice ragged. "We've made a business arrangement. That's all."

"Yes."

But even though he admitted the folly of kissing this woman, it didn't stop him from moving inward to the hollow beneath her collarbone.

"We'll consider this a rehearsal of sorts."

The gruffness of her tone was like a bare hand against his nerves.

"Hell, yes."

"Can you keep up this sort of emotional involvement whenever they're near?"

"I don't think that will be a problem."

Then, not wanting to talk any more, he took her lips with his again, kissing her with an intensity that bordered on obsession. He couldn't remember the last time any woman had made him so mindlessly needy before. Not Amanda, to be sure. Not even Liz. No. Dana Shaw had some sort of magical effect on him that made him forget who she was and why she was with him. There was only this moment. This kiss. This embrace.

Her fingers tunneled beneath his sweater, encountering the muscles of his stomach. He couldn't avoid the twitch of his stomach or the molten fire that spread into his groin. Nor could he ignore the groan that ripped from his mouth into her own.

It was Dana who wrenched away. "We should get upstairs."

"Mm-hmm." He was trailing his tongue down her neck, circling her Adam's apple.

"As soon as anyone realizes we've stopped..."

She didn't finish what she'd been about to say; she merely groaned, sinking her fingers into his hair and bringing him up for a deep, enervating kiss. One filled with passion and promise. One that he would never be able to forget—and moreover, would never be able to match.

Their anxious movements caused the elevator car to shimmy, but neither of them paid it any mind. The only regret was that the cramped space offered very little space for any real maneuvering or—

"I told you she loved the man. They *must* be in love to make such a spectacle of themselves."

Sean jerked upright at the raspy comment. His surroundings rushed into focus with stunning alacrity, giving him an all-too-clear picture of the woman he'd hiked onto the elevator railing, the open door and the three elderly ladies staring aghast at them both.

"In my day, we left such intimacies in the bedroom," April continued, flicking her lighter and putting the flame to the tip of her green cigarillo.

"I think it's romantic," June murmured with an all-knowing grin.

Mae made a choking sound and turned away.

Blinking, Sean tried to gather his scattered thoughts. Somehow, the elevator had made its way to its proper destination—all without him being aware of the ascent. The gilded doors had opened wide, and the three elderly ladies were still watching him as if he were some sort of masher intent on seducing innocent maids.

Which was what he was, he supposed.

Although, he didn't think the maid he'd chosen was all *that* innocent. She'd known just how to affect *him.*

April dragged deep on the cigarillo and turned her attention to her niece. "Don't you think you should get down now?"

Sean reluctantly backed away, and Dana's feet returned to the rose-patterned carpet. She smoothed her hair, then touched her lips. At some point, she'd been wearing a deep, natural shade of lipstick. Sean could only pray it wasn't smeared all over his own face.

"If this is a bad time for dinner," April announced, "we could postpone the event."

Dana clutched his hand. "No, no. We're looking forward to it."

April shot them both a disbelieving glance. "Doubt it."

Aunt April had changed her beige shirt dress for a sheath and cardigan of the same indeterminate color of beige. Other than the cigarillo she smoked, her only ornamentation for the evening was the beaded set of clips that held the sweater over her shoulders.

Aunt Mae, on the other hand, had kept her sunglasses—even in the dim light of the hall. Her stole had been exchanged for an embroidered net dinner jacket, and the beaded gown had gone from ivory to black.

Aunt June, ever the Easter egg, was bedecked in a sequined caftan with dolman sleeves that looked like a butterfly's wings whenever she moved her arms—something she was prone to do a great deal in order to keep the scrawny, mottled Chihuahua she held at bay as it wriggled and yapped and growled in Sean's direction.

"Are you finished?" April inquired, swinging her cigarillo wide and leaving a trail of smoke like an accusing finger. "Dinner is getting cold."

Sean saw the way a faint color was creeping up Dana's neck and into her cheeks. Not knowing why he felt compelled to help her find a graceful way out of the situation, but knowing he had to do something, he slid his arm into the crook at her waist and hugged her close.

"I suppose we can't go much farther than that until the wedding, can we?" he murmured with a wink.

Dana stiffened.

Aunt April scowled.

June beamed.

Mae uttered a choked cry.

"What's for supper?" Sean asked with the most charming grin he could summon.

None of the elderly women answered. Instead, they turned their backs to him and marched en masse in the direction of an open door at the far end of the corridor. Through it all, the dog—Babbette, he supposed—glared at him over June's shoulder, yapping and growling and baring her teeth.

"Watch out for the dog," Dana murmured as the two of them followed.

It was the only warning she was allowed to give.

They stepped into a gracious apartment with ten-foot ceilings and ornate period woodwork. Other than that, there was no sign of the glamorous thirties when the building must have been constructed. Instead, everything was beige—couch, walls, chairs, drapes and rugs—all of it modeled with a box-shaped sparseness that proclaimed it had been purchased about the same time Jackie Kennedy was renovating the White House. Over it all was a layer of clear plastic—plastic runners, cushion covers and table-cloths.

"Have a seat."

Sean hesitated, unsure where he was supposed to sit. The protective shields shrouding everything in the room made him hesitant to touch anything for fear of disturbing the museumlike perfection to be found underneath its layer of vinyl. Even the room smelled like a public museum, the faint odor of cigarillo smoke mingling with the sharper tang of new plastic.

"Where?" he asked.

June glared at him. "At the table."

"Oh." He offered another quick grin and made his way to the Formica-topped table and pedestal chairs, which had probably been purchased during the Johnson administration.

The cushion protectors crackled as he took his seat. Since his arm was around Dana's neck, he all but pulled Dana into the chair positioned next to him.

The aunts reluctantly selected their own places, April at the head of the table and Mae and June opposite Dana and Sean.

"Get rid of the beast."

Sean started, then realized that April was referring to the Chihuahua.

June pouted, stroking the animal's head. "Babbette has very nice table manners, April. You know that. I've taught her to—"

"I don't care if you give her a wig and call her Shirley Temple, that animal is a *dog,* June. A mean, nasty, horrible, yippy dog. I will not have it eating at my table.''

June's jaw squared, and she clutched the animal a little tighter to her breast, causing it to squirm even more.

''Put it on the floor. Now,'' April warned.

June offered a persecuted sigh, murmuring a stream of babyish prattle she set the animal on the floor. Her toenails scrabbled on the vinyl runner, then she disappeared beneath the tablecloth.

''Well, then,'' April stated, planting her palms wide on either side of her plate as if ready to give a speech—or a sermon.

Sean quickly dipped his head, sure that the gruff woman meant to give grace.

Instead, she shouted, ''Madison!''

There was a crash from one of the inner rooms. The swinging door behind the table opened, and a grizzled, balding head appeared.

''Time to serve,'' April reminded him.

The old man shuffled back into the kitchen, leaving the door flapping behind him.

April retrieved her napkin, snapped it open with a flick of her wrist and settled it over her lap. ''So, Sean—may I call you Sean?''

''Yes, ma'am,'' he answered, wrestling his hand free from Dana's grip so that he could reach for his own napkin, a thick linen affair that had been ironed and starched so that it settled over his legs with the grace of a two-by-four.

"What do you do?"

"When?"

April dragged her bread plate closer and flicked her ashes into the center. "For a living?"

"I work the family ranch."

"Whose family?"

He thought that point had been obvious. "Mine. We have seven hundred acres of farm and pasture-land that have been worked by the O'Malley generations since the late nineteenth century."

"What is your gross income each year?"

"Aunt April!" Dana exclaimed.

April dipped her head to peer through her thick lenses. "It's a question that needs to be asked. Why be coy?"

Sean waved away Dana's objections. "I suppose it's only logical that your aunts would be worried about your welfare, darling. After all, we *are* to be married."

Dana's lashes widened ever so slightly at the endearment, and he took the opportunity to slip his arm around her shoulders and hug her close. There was an element of danger in the embrace. He knew he had to have a clear head to deal with the situation, and by touching Dana, he found that echoes of the passion they'd shared in the elevator threatened to flood his brain. Nevertheless, he didn't move away. He couldn't. He didn't want to.

"You were about to tell us about your income," April prompted.

"Yes." Sean cleared his throat, assuming a businesslike mien. "We gross a six-digit amount, but those profits are dispersed among my father, oldest sister and I. They also help to support my other seven siblings."

"There are nine of you?" It was the first time Mae had spoken that evening. She whipped off her sunglasses, stared at him and repeated, *"Nine?"*

"Yes, ma'am."

She swiftly replaced the sunglasses, drained her water glass, then reached for the wine bottle near the centerpiece of hothouse daisies.

April rapped Mae's knuckles, and she subsided into her chair again, minus the liquor she'd craved.

Somewhere near his ankles, Sean could feel the warm breath of the Chihuahua and hear its faint growling.

"So many children," June murmured.

"Yes, ma'am." Sean absently twined a finger around a lock of Dana's hair, absorbing its texture, its weight. "My mother passed on about two years ago—complications due to diabetes. Just a year later, my father was involved in a farm accident. Unfortunately, he slipped into a coma. He's being cared for at a medical facility near our home."

"What kind of accident was it, Mr. O'Malley?" June inquired, her eyes moist at the lashes.

"PTO."

"I don't understand," April demanded. "Did it sink? Like in that movie about John F. Kennedy?"

Sean had to resist the urge to laugh. "No, ma'am. A PTO is a piece of farm equipment."

"I see."

It was clear she didn't.

"It's a mechanism that—"

April interrupted him when he would have explained. "Tell me, Mr. O'Malley, do you intend for our niece to bear nine children?"

This time, it was Dana who was reaching for her water glass. Her shoulders had grown incredibly stiff under Sean's arm, and he wondered what she was thinking.

"No, ma'am."

He nearly smiled when Dana's posture eased slightly. He couldn't resist adding, "We were thinking more along the line of five or six."

Dana choked.

Mae gasped.

June clapped.

April snorted. "Don't you think that's a bit excessive in light of the world in this day and age?"

Sean pulled Dana even closer, settling her neck into the crook of his arm.

"Not when two people love each other like we do, ma'am."

Mae made a mewling sound and reached for the wine bottle again, this time managing to avoid her sister's interference. As soon as she'd filled her glass, June held out her own, but rather than looking shocked, there was a decided gleam in her eyes.

"You must be a very...strong man to consider fathering so many children."

Sean wasn't sure if he liked the way she said "strong." It sounded almost...lurid the way she lingered over each letter.

"Tell me—" June leaned closer, her fingers stroking the stem of her wineglass "—have you ever been sculpted? Nude?"

"Aunt June!" Dana gulped.

Sean ignored the outburst at the table. "No, ma'am."

"But he's been featured in a calendar." Dana spoke for the first time in several minutes. Unfortunately, Sean wished she'd remained silent on that particular subject.

"Is it true?" June breathed.

"Yes, ma'am. This past year."

"What month?"

"January."

"Ooh." It was obvious that such a fact made him more acceptable in June's eyes than the O'Malley family's gross income.

"And how were you photographed? Naked?"

Dana was the first to speak. "He was more than adequately dressed, Aunt June. They put him in the bottom half of his bunker gear."

"Oh, my-y-y," June drawled. "Just the bottoms? Can I have a copy?"

"June Marie Flowers, get hold of yourself, do you hear?" April snapped. "Our goal here is to discover this man's intentions, not titillate your artistic libido."

June straightened in her chair, but it was obvious from her all-knowing smile that she was far from dissuaded.

"Beast," April snapped.

Sean started, sure that the one-word epithet had been a reaction to June's attitude. Instead, April bent at the waist and scooped the Chihuahua from the floor. She had grabbed a corner of the tablecloth in her mouth and was growling and shaking it from side to side in ferocious glee.

"Come get this animal, June."

June complied, making her way around the gathered group with a bit more hip-swaying than Sean thought necessary.

"Is Mommy's itsy-bitsy Babby-wabby being a naughty girl, hmm?" she cooed, taking the scrawny mutt from her sister. As she pried the animal's jaws loose, she uttered a mishmash of endearments that made even the dog's eyes roll. Finally, she managed to untangle the cloth from her teeth and return to her seat.

"Take the beast back to your room."

June shook her head, still tickling the animal under her chin and babbling to her. "She can't be left alone, April, and you know it. Her psychiatrist said so."

A psychiatrist? For a dog?

"Then take care of her."

"She'll behave if you let her eat with us."

April sucked in her breath, pursed her lips, then exhaled. "Fine. Fine! Just keep her away from the wine. I won't have a repeat of the last time she ate at this table." She offered a stern look of warning, then bellowed, "Madison, where is our food?"

AS FAR AS DANA WAS concerned, the entire evening went downhill from that moment on.

Babbette was set at the foot of the table. Propped on a stack of phone books, a frilly baby's bib secured around her neck, she panted and surveyed the group, then continued to take dainty bites of the salmon mousse and laps of cream poured into a saucer.

It was one of the most bizarre evenings Dana had ever endured—and since she'd lived with her aunts' eccentricities for most of her life, that was saying something. Course by course, minute by minute, the triplets grilled Sean for information while he, on the other hand, grew more and more demonstrative, kissing Dana's neck, her hand, the top of her head, and referring to her as "dear," "sweetheart" and "my little lamb."

She could only be glad that the camera crew hadn't been present. If Rick and Adam had recorded the event, she knew that she would never be taken seriously in the news world again.

But then again, there was an even more serious side effect to his behavior. The spontaneous embrace in the elevator had been enough of a shock to her system. It had wrenched her from her casual belief that this week could be simple. That she could remain in control of this whole charade.

Wrong. Wrong, wrong, *wrong*. What had occurred in the elevator had been enough to convince her that she was beyond mere attraction. What she'd experienced in his company had been more sudden and more elemental than anything she'd ever encountered. It hadn't helped that he'd spent the evening touching her, caressing her, all beneath the watchful eyes of her aunts. Dana kept vacillating between wishing his attitude toward her was real, and fearing that, in some small measure, his behavior wasn't entirely an act.

After all, he'd responded to *her* in the elevator, too.

Passionately.

Intently.

Completely.

At long last, even though Dana feared such an event would never take place, Aunt April finally stood. Pushing her dessert plate and coffee cup out of the way, she announced, "The two of you must be tired."

It was quite clear that the royal audience was over and the plebes were being dismissed.

Sean rose to his feet, and Dana struggled to do the same even as her legs reacted in a rubbery, weak-kneed manner that could only be the result of the nerve-racking evening and not the stroking of his fingers against her neck.

"The three of you must be exhausted, as well," Dana commented in an attempt to cover her awkwardness. "What with all the preparations you've been making..."

But the elderly women weren't looking at her; they were regarding Sean, testing his character.

"We've assigned you both a room in the guest wing."

"Room?" Dana echoed, having caught the word over all of the others. *"Room?"*

Aunt April shot her a chiding glance. "We may have been raised in another era—" she began.

"But we pride ourselves on being modern minded," June interrupted. "We were able to secure the honeymoon suite for you."

Again, a mewl of distress from Mae.

June jabbed her in the ribs with her elbow. "We all agree it's for the best, don't we, Mae?"

Mae bit her lip and looked away.

Aunt April was pushing them to the door, taking a key from her pocket. "This is yours—there's only one, I'm afraid, so you'll have to orchestrate your comings and goings."

Dana was still grappling with the fact that her aunts had secured *a* room. *One.*

"When you get to the bottom floor, make a right, a left and a right. It's the last door at the end of the hall."

Vaguely, she saw the way Sean took the key.

"Goodnight, dear." Aunt April bussed her cheek.

Mae cast a glance in Sean's direction, and her lips tightened. When she leaned close to Dana for a parting hug, she whispered, "Watch him. Ramone can't be trusted."

Then June held her tightly, murmuring, "Lucky girl. I bet he's a tiger in bed. Grrr-rarr."

Try as she might, Dana couldn't prevent the scalding heat from easing up her neck to her cheeks. Then, before she knew what had really happened, she was ushered into the hall, the last few evening salutations were exchanged and the door snapped closed.

Leaving her alone.

With a man who suddenly looked angry enough to pound nails with his bare hands.

Chapter Five

The door had barely closed behind them before Sean's hand dropped away from the hollow of her back and he drilled her with a piercing stare.

"One room?" he drawled, his tone less than pleased. "We're supposed to sleep together in *one* room?"

"Shh!" Dana cast a glance in either direction, smiling vaguely at an elderly couple letting themselves into a suite down the hall.

Ignoring the antique elevator that waited for its next load, she marched to the stairs, knowing that Sean would follow. After all, what else could he do?

Sure enough, she heard him prowling along behind her, and inwardly, she breathed a silent sigh of relief. In his current mood, she wouldn't have put it past him to force some sort of confrontation in the corridor.

As they walked, she could feel his eyes burning into the back of her head, reminding her all too eloquently that soon she would be sequestered with this man in the honeymoon suite—the *honeymoon* suite, for heaven's sake. Why a retirement village would need a honeymoon suite, she didn't know, but she *did* know that after their encounter in the elevator and her own spineless reaction to her aunt's inquisition, it was time Dana took control of this situation. She'd bought and paid for this man's services as her fiancé. It was time he was reminded of that.

Just as it was time he was reminded to keep at arm's length from his employer.

It didn't take long to follow her aunts' directions and locate the room they were to use. The fact that the door had been painted a brilliant red didn't hurt, either.

"Give me the key, please." Dana didn't look at him. She merely held out her hand, palm up, expecting him to comply.

"Why don't you just tell them that we don't want to sleep together?"

She shot him a scathing glance. "We're supposed to be engaged."

"So we're saving such a practice for after the wedding."

"I will not argue with them. I will not make them any more suspicious of this relationship than they already are." The words were uttered in a clipped, succinct manner, but as far as she could see, they had no effect on him whatsoever.

"The key," she said again.

He inhaled, making his chest expand, and prompting her to wonder suddenly what had ever happened to his coat. She hadn't seen it since she'd pushed it off his shoulders to the floor of the elevator.

Sean slapped the key into her palm and planted his hands on his hips, glaring in Dana's direction as she fumbled with the lock.

"Tell me, Dana. Did you plan all this? After our...experience in the elevator, did you decide to arrange for us to spend the evening in the same room?"

"Don't flatter yourself."

But the clichéd response lost some of its sting when she realized that at any other time, any other place, she might have been tempted to do just that.

What in the world was coming over her? Had she completely lost her mind?

Throwing the portal wide, Dana waited for Sean to precede her.

"I hope you don't intend for me to carry you over the threshold," he said.

"Don't be absurd."

Offering one more grimace, he moved into the room. Steeling herself, Dana did the same.

A weak sliver of light pierced the blinds, revealing that their belongings had been gathered from the roadster and stacked neatly at the foot of the bed. Good. At least she wouldn't have to brave the storm outside—although she was sure there would be plenty of chilly weather in the honeymoon suite.

She was reaching for the light switch when she heard Sean growling, "What the hell...?"

The room was flooded with a buttery warmth. Dana's eyes focused, blinked, then squinted at the sight laid out before her.

The Greycliff Retirement Village had chosen a jungle motif. A *jungle* motif.

The walls were lined with torches that flickered with an artificial feebleness, while behind them, the surfaces had been painted with twisted foliage and heathen masks. In the center of the room, the massive bed featured a headboard of carved teak and a spread of deep green and black. The floors were scattered with artificial animal rugs, low divans and enough tasseled pillows to make a pasha jealous.

"Good hell, Almighty," Sean muttered under his breath.

Dana could only blink in astonishment, sure that she was dreaming, that what she was seeing couldn't possibly be true.

Then Sean turned to face her, his eyes burning with a blue fire—one that she sensed wasn't entirely due to his irritation.

She tried to squelch the sensation, but a shiver of exhilaration raced down her spine. She was about to spend the evening here, alone, with a man who had his own brand of earthy allure. A man that she wouldn't entirely mind being Tarzan to her Jane.

He must have read at least a portion of her thoughts, because he took a step toward her. Just one step. But it was enough to cause her breath to hitch in her throat.

When he reached out, cupping her chin, she couldn't prevent the way she melted into the simple touch. Her mind screamed for control, but her body...

Her body had become a traitor.

"Are you sure this is what you want?"

She wasn't even sure what he meant by such a question.

"Do you really want to spend the night alone with me? In one room? One bed?"

The thought was enough to make her body warmer than she would have thought possible.

Distantly, she heard a knock on the door and she thanked her lucky stars that someone had seen fit to interrupt them. Otherwise, she feared she would have thrown caution to the wind.

Pulling herself away from him took every ounce of will she possessed.

"Who is it?" Her voice was so garbled, she feared she would not be understood.

"Rick."

Damn. The last thing she needed was to remind Sean about the camera crew.

Opening the door, she tried to keep her body between Rick and her "roommate."

"Yes?"

"What time will you be needing us tomorrow?"

She shrugged. "I'll let you know."

"Great. We're in room 6. It's in the east wing."

"Thanks, Rick."

She was about to shut the door again when he slapped the panels on his end and held out a slip of paper. "A call came for O'Malley. Since we couldn't find you, I took a message."

She took the paper, praying Rick would move away before he had a chance to see the jungle motif.

But when he snickered, she knew she hadn't been successful.

"Have fun, bwana," he chortled, then closed the door himself.

Dana stood where she was, not moving, allowing several beats of silence to thrum in the room around her.

She must not allow Sean to touch her again.

If he did, she would be finished.

"Here," she said abruptly, holding out the slip and moving to the bed, where she could busy herself with her suitcase.

She heard the paper crackle, then nothing. Nothing at all.

Her head rose, and she found Sean staring at some point above the far wall. A muscle was working furiously in his cheek.

"Is there a phone I can use?"

She pointed to the nightstand. "Just dial the number, it's an outside line."

He nodded, lifting the receiver and punching a series of buttons he obviously knew by heart.

Dana hefted her suitcase onto the bed, trying not to eavesdrop. But the room didn't allow for much privacy—and to be quite honest, she had this unaccountable need to discover why he'd become so cool, so tense.

"Yeah, it's me," he said into the phone.

He listened, saying nothing for several minutes. Dana did her best to concentrate on the zipper of her soft-sided bag.

"What time?" he asked curtly. "Fine. I'll be there—yes, I will, Carol. Just leave it to me."

The other party said something more, then he signed off with a firm "Goodbye, Carol."

He replaced the receiver with a little more force than necessary, then stood with his hands on his hips, glaring down at it.

"Is something wrong?" Dana asked after several moments.

When he turned to face her, there was no hiding his anger and frustration. "When I signed on with that bachelor auction, I agreed to one week of service. Granted, when my sisters volunteered my help, they left the terms a bit vague. Even so, I did not agree to become some sort of peep show for your public admirers."

So they were back to the issue of the camera crew.

"If you didn't want such a thing to occur, you should have been more specific about which activities you wished to avoid."

His gaze flicked to the bed and back again. "Somehow, I'm sure that the Make a Wish Foundation wouldn't agree to some twisted form of stud service."

She gasped. "I never—"

"Didn't you?"

"No!"

Sean's voice had grown steadily louder and she hurried to silence him.

"And keep your voice down. There are people trying to sleep here. *Old* people."

He stabbed the air in front of her chest with a finger. "Don't you tell me there are old people here. I just spent the better part of the evening playing the fawning suitor for your aunts."

"Speaking of which, don't you think that you were laying it on a little thick? All that touching and kissing and cooing."

"You wanted me to be convincing."

"I didn't want you to set the date for May 5!"

"I was trying to be thorough."

"You were trying to be annoying, and you know it."

His lips twitched slightly at that remark, but even the reminder of his audacity wasn't enough to dent his ill humor. "Obviously, it worked. Your aunts adore me."

She huffed in indignation. "Hardly. Aunt Mae warned me about trusting you."

"Your aunt Mae wishes *she* was the one spending the night with me in this room."

Dana knew that was true, but she resented the fact that he'd found it necessary to point it out.

"Nevertheless, they've arranged for us to use this...suite, and we're stuck with it."

"Why?"

"Because if either of us moves out of here, it would hardly give credence to our protestations of undying love."

She flung the top to her suitcase open. "We'll just have to make the best of things. I'll take the bed, and you can take the couch. That should reassure whatever sensibilities I've offended on your part."

"I don't think so."

His comment was so soft, so simple, it took a moment to sink into her brain. When it did, she lifted an eyebrow. "I beg your pardon?"

"I don't think so," he repeated. "You take the couch. I'll take the bed."

She straightened to full height, tilting her head so that she could peer up at him with that same intimidating stare she used on recalcitrant interview subjects. She even allowed a beat of silence, then lifted one eyebrow imperiously.

"As you so pointedly reminded me, *I* was the one who paid for your services this week—more than once. Therefore, I'll be the one to take the bed."

His lips thinned. "The contract said seven *days*—"

"It said a week, Mr. O'Malley. A week. There was no stipulation made as to night or day, merely one *full* week."

He didn't like the fact that she'd won this particular argument, but when he exhaled and reached for his duffel bag, she was relieved. After all, her aunts might have the ability to transform her into a spineless adolescent bent on approval, but that did not mean that Sean O'Malley could expect the same.

As long as she could keep him from touching her. If he touched her, she was doomed.

Sean disappeared into the bathroom. She heard his duffel drop to the floor and a muffled "Great, bloody *hell!*" Then the door slammed closed.

Dana didn't bother to ask what he'd found to inspire such a reaction. Judging by what she'd seen of the main rooms, she didn't think she could take any more surprises. Not for a minute or two.

Sighing, she began to root through her suitcase. She was determined to treat this entire evening as if there were nothing at all unusual about it. So she and that man—that earthy, overwhelming calendar man—would be sharing a room. Big deal. It wasn't as if she'd never done such a thing before. Granted, the quarters were intimate, the circumstances odd and the man—well . . .

Intriguing.

Strong.

Infinitely masculine.

Stop it!

Annoyed at her own dithering, she reached for the makeup bag she always tucked into the upper right-hand corner.

Nothing. There was nothing there but a clear sack holding the shoes she would wear to the birthday ball.

Damn. That meant she would have to search through the entire suitcase.

But five minutes later, she was still empty-handed and the contents of her suitcase were strewed untidily over her bed.

Frantically, she tried to think where she'd seen her makeup bag last. She remembered taking it into the bathroom at the last minute while she'd brushed her teeth. Once she'd finished, she'd dropped toothpaste and her brush inside and...

Fred had come to the door to announce the roadster had been delivered. Thaddeus had handed her the bag of workout clothes and reminded her of the time.

Then she'd dashed from her apartment, leaving the men in charge of loading her bags...

And forgetting to pack the makeup kit she'd left on the counter.

No! No, no, *no*. She couldn't go a week without her cosmetics. Not with road travel impossible. Not with the birthday bash scheduled.

Not while she was sharing a room with Sean O'Malley.

Rushing to her purse, she dumped it onto the bedspread, hurriedly rummaging through the contents. To her infinite relief, she found a tube of lipstick, blusher and the tiny traveling toothbrush she'd put in the zippered compartment for just such emergencies. But that did not offer her shampoo, conditioner, a brush or even toothpaste. And what about soap? She had no soap! No antiperspirant. No dental floss.

The bathroom door opened at that moment, and Sean strode out.

"I hope the use of the honeymoon lair includes a maid," he remarked dryly, seeing the mess she'd created.

Dana swallowed against the sudden dryness of her throat. His chest was bare. That firm, muscular chest. Aunt June was right—he must lift weights of some sort because she could see each ridge and valley of his form as if it had been carefully honed and cast in bronze. He was water dappled, his hair wet from a shower. The clean scent of soap and male filled the room.

Needing to say something, anything, to banish the shivering expectancy that had filled the silence, Dana asked, "Forget your pajamas?"

She gestured to the jeans riding low on his hips, the snap unfastened to show a peek of white from his briefs.

He was raking one hand through his hair, but paused long enough to fix her with a rich stare. "I don't wear pajamas."

What was she supposed to say in response to that?

As she was searching for something to break the quiet, Dana's eyes fell on the shaving kit he cradled in the crook of his elbow. When she saw the soap, still damp and maintaining a streak of suds, she latched on to that spot with an almost potent hunger.

"Listen, I've forgotten my makeup kit. Could I borrow your soap?"

When he didn't immediately respond, she looked up to find that his eyebrows had climbed a fraction of an inch.

"You don't have soap?"

"No." She wiped her hands on her thighs. "I could also use some shampoo."

"Oh, really? Anything else?"

"Mmm-hmm," she admitted uncomfortably. "Toothpaste. A brush."

"I have a comb."

"It'll do."

"It will, huh?"

He was being so agreeable, so helpful, that it made her nervous. Somehow, she knew it would not be so easy to gain her request. That assumption was confirmed by the wicked smile that spread over his features.

Sinking into a leather arm chair for two, he lifted the comb from his kit and held it up to the light as if it were a faceted gem.

"What are you willing to give me for the use of this little item?"

"Surely you aren't suggesting that I bargain for it."

His grin was absolutely potent. "You were the one who insisted we abide by the letter of our contract. I don't remember the use of personal-grooming articles being mentioned anywhere."

"I suppose you'll want the bed in trade?"

"Not in that condition."

Huffing in irritation, she gathered her clothing in her arms and transferred the bundle to the couch.

"Is that satisfactory?"

He moved from the chair to the bed with sinuous grace. After wriggling as if to find the most comfortable spot—smack dab in the middle of the mattress—he dragged the pillows under his head and sighed, closing his eyes.

"Are you quite finished?" she asked through clenched teeth, wondering why she hadn't bothered to purchase a bachelor who would be more docile, more obedient.

His eyes opened, and his grin widened even more as he focused on the ceiling. "Oh, look! There's a mirror!"

"Are you finished?" she demanded again.

"I suppose."

He tossed the comb in her direction.

"What about the rest of the things I need?"

"The rest?" he asked with an innocence that didn't match the devilish sparkle of his eyes. "You're going to have to offer me something else for the rest."

She threw the comb onto the pile of clothing behind her. "I was bidding for everything when I suggested the bed."

"You didn't make that fact clear."

"I didn't know I had to. You don't think I'd offer the bed in exchange for one measly item, do you?"

"That *was* my impression, yes."

She huffed in impatience. "Then what do you want for the rest of it—for anything, *anything* in your shaving kit or suitcase, I might have a need for over the next week?"

"You want my clothes, too?"

"I might."

He shrugged. "Fine with me. How much are you willing to pay?"

"You want money?" she asked incredulously.

He shook his head. "Something for charity will be fine. But I want it paid in advance."

"Advance?"

"Now that I know you're a member of the press, I don't trust you to keep your word."

Grumbling a host of epithets under her breath, she snatched her wallet from the pile of things on the floor. "The Make a Wish Foundation is going to love you," she muttered, snapping her wallet open. "Will a check do?"

He tugged the pillows more firmly beneath his neck so that he could watch her write. "As long as you have two forms of identification."

She shot him a withering glance, but it didn't seem to have much effect. "How much?"

"An even thousand should do it."

"A *thousand!*"

"You'll have to admit it's a bargain. Only—" he thought a moment "—a hundred and sixty-six dollars a day and some change."

"That's robbery."

"You could borrow some toiletries from your aunts."

She snapped her wallet shut. "I think I will."

He waited until she was midway to the door. "Of course, they might think it strange that you didn't just get it from me. Your beloved."

She opened her mouth to make some pithy remark, closed it and retrieved her wallet. Without speaking, she scrawled out the amount, ripped the check free, then stood and threw it in his direction. The paper fluttered in the air, then landed in the middle of his stomach. In that perfect hollow made between his hipbones and his ribs.

What would it feel like to put her hand there?

To explore the corrugated muscles of his stomach...

To place her lips on that warm skin and...

Dana jerked her thoughts back to a safer path. She mustn't think about that. She mustn't.

"Well?" she demanded stiffly, praying the wayward images hadn't somehow been conveyed to the man on the bed.

He pushed the shaving kit toward her. "Knock yourself out."

Snatching the case into the crook of her elbow, she gathered her robe, pajamas and underwear, then crossed to the bathroom.

"Oh, and Dana..."

Her head dropped in defeat. She'd been so close. Two more seconds, and the door would have shut firmly behind her.

"Yes?" she asked, not turning, not looking at him. But such a course of action was worse, so much worse. She could see him in the mirror on the bathroom wall—or rather, she could see most of him, from knee to throat. Nevertheless, she couldn't keep her gaze from straying to his hips, to the muscles that led her gaze to the placket of his jeans and beyond, where a very masculine bulge had been outlined by some freak angle of a light over his head.

"Watch out for the loincloths."

Again, she was forced to summon every scrap of control she could muster to bring her imagination to heel.

"Loincloths?"

"Mmm-hmm."

She saw him stretch like a well-fed cat, then roll toward her and cock a knee in such a way that the placket of his jeans threatened to expose a bit more of his briefs than before.

"What loincloths?" She had to force her lips to say the words.

"There's a pair of them hanging next to the shower. Heaven only knows if they're supplied with the room, or if the last happy couple left them here."

His only answer was the slam of the door.

Sean chuckled, wondering where his anger had gone, his suspicion, his irritation. After his wrangling with Dana Shaw, it had momentarily disappeared.

But as the minutes ticked by, he couldn't keep his worry from returning. Carol had sounded so distraught on the phone, informing him that social services would be paying a visit to the ranch the following Tuesday. Even though Sean was a blood relative and the logical choice as guardian to his three youngest sisters, the legalities hadn't been completely finalized as yet. He still needed a positive report from the assigned caseworker.

Which meant he had keep his face from appearing on the evening news.

No matter what it took to do so.

Chapter Six

Sean's vow to circumvent Dana's efforts to interview him returned full force the moment he woke to find the lens of a camera not three inches from his face.

"Kidding, just kidding," Rick Bermen announced, swinging the equipment away just when Sean's hand closed around the base of his throat.

Sean was not amused.

Sensing that Sean wasn't about to be placated, Rick said quickly, "Dana sent me to come get you. She's been working with her aunts since dawn, but she thinks it's time you made an appearance."

A knock at the door was enough to send Sean grabbing for his jeans and Rick heading for the bathroom. Why the cameraman felt it necessary to hide from whoever had come to see him, Sean didn't know. In fact, he didn't care, he thought as he raked his fingers through his hair and massaged at the tension already knotting the back of his neck.

Slipping into his jeans, he fastened all but the top snap, then padded to the door and braced himself against the wall with one palm. Peering around the edge of the lintel, he found an elderly woman waiting on the other side.

Garish colors.

Pink hair.

June.

"Oh, my," she breathed, confirming her identity with such a heated sigh that he wished he'd taken the time to don more than his jeans.

"I really must sculpt you. I *must*."

"I don't think—"

"You'd be wonderful!" She took a step back, touching thumbs and peering at him through the frame of her hands as if she were some sort of movie director. "You could use that pose—that *very* pose. But the pants would have to go. I only sculpt nudes, you know."

Sean was at a loss as to how to respond to that. "I don't think—"

"No, *really!*" she insisted. "I'm quite good. You'll find some of my work in the recreation hall." She edged closer, lowering her voice as if confiding in him. "Some of the residents here dabble in painting or writing or the latest artsy-craftsy nonsense, but I am truly *passionate* about my work."

She gripped his arm with such fervor that Sean could only reply, "I'm sure you are."

June brightened as if he'd just announced she'd won the lottery.

"Then you'll consider the idea?"

No. Hell, no. But somehow, he thought such a blunt refusal would only cause her to concentrate on changing his mind. He said instead, "I'll think about it."

"Marvelous. Marvelous!" She finally released him to clap her hands.

"Was there something else you needed, June?"

"Aunt June. Please. After all, we're to be family!"

"Aunt June," he complied, already angling the door in front of his body.

"I've been sent to tell you that April is waiting for you in the recreation room."

"April? I thought Dana—"

"Never mind her. She's busy at the moment. But April needs your help—quite desperately."

"Really?"

"Oh, yes."

"Then I suppose I should get ready."

She didn't move, but merely narrowed her eyes and began to inspect him from head to toe. "Bronze, I think," she murmured to herself. "Or maybe... papier-mâché."

Since she didn't seem inclined to leave—and he wasn't ready for an audience while he put on his clothes—Sean closed the door. Shaking his head in disbelief, he gathered a clean set of jeans, a white button-down shirt and his socks. Banging on the bathroom door with his fist, he said, "Get out of there. I've got to get dressed."

Fifteen minutes later, he was striding down the main corridor on the ground level of the village complex, following the discreet signs that pointed him in the direction of the recreation room.

"Do you really have to follow me so closely?" he asked under his breath when Bermen trailed his every step.

"Yep. Just pretend I'm not here."

Sean resisted the urge to roll his eyes. "Yeah, right."

At long last, he saw the double doors. Stepping into an elegant lounge, he stopped and stared. Somewhere on the periphery of his vision, he noted the dozen or so guests milling about the area—some of them reading or watching television or playing Ping-Pong. But what caught his attention and held it fast was the huge statue placed on a dais in the center of the room.

Behind him, he heard Bermen stumble. "Oh...my...gosh..." the cameraman said slowly, and Sean tore his gaze away long enough to see Bermen focusing on the piece, zooming in on it, scaling it from head to toe.

Sean's own stare returned to the bronze study with the strength of a boomerang. A pair of lovers was entwined in a passionate embrace that left little—if anything—to the imagination.

"Get a load of that fellow's..." Bermen began, then stopped, as if realizing he was surrounded by a group of octogenarians. "Eyes," he finished lamely.

Despite himself, Sean felt a heat creeping up his neck. June had been right. She was good. Very, very good. And if she thought she was going to parade Sean's private attributes for all the world to see, she had another think coming!

"Over here, boy."

The raspy command could only have come from one person, and Sean was glad for the diversion. April was seated at a round gaming table, three other men serving as her opponents.

"Have a seat," she said, waving a cigarillo in the general direction of the only available chair.

Sean hesitated, but judging by the determined glitter of the eyes that bored into him, he didn't really have a choice.

As soon as he was settled, the rest of the group ogled him with a great deal of interest.

"This is Sean O'Malley," April said. "The one I told you about."

It was apparent from their reactions that whatever she'd said hadn't bowled them over.

"He thinks he's going to marry my niece."

One man wagged his head from side to side as if he were amazed by such a folly.

"He also says he can't play bridge."

A woman with silver hair put a hand to her heart as if pained.

"But he claims to have some skill at poker."

As Sean recalled, he hadn't claimed any such thing, but it didn't appear as if he was going to have a say in the matter.

April took a deck of cards, fanned it onto the table, flipped them face up, then gathered them together and shuffled them with a croupier's finesse.

"Cut the cards," she said, extending them to him.

IT WAS NEARING lunchtime when Dana looked up from the hemline she'd been marking on Aunt Mae's latest gown and realized that she hadn't seen Sean since she'd left him early that morning.

"There you are, Aunt Mae. Are there any more dresses you need fixed?"

Mae was staring into the three-way mirror that had been erected in one corner of her bedroom. Even in Dana's company, she wore the thick-rimmed sunglasses—which made it all but impossible for her to see her own reflection.

"I don't know..." she began hesitantly, and Dana sighed, hoping she had the patience to endure another change of clothing.

Dana had arrived downstairs to a terrible fuss early that morning. The weather had deteriorated into a first-rate blizzard, and since the first of the birthday activities was scheduled to take place that evening, her aunts had been in a dither about what to do. Only half of the out-of-town guests had arrived, and it didn't appear that those still en route would be allowed to drive through the canyon. It had been up to Dana to calm the elderly women and insist that the celebration be held as planned, since the majority of the guests would be in attendance. April and June had been easy to sway, but Mae...

Mae had begun to cry, sure that this would be the worst birthday ever. The *worst*.

Hoping to cheer her up, Dana had volunteered to help her choose something to wear for the newsreel marathon scheduled later that night.

The idea had been a mistake.

Aunt Mae was passionate about fashion and owned—not a closet full of clothes, but several rooms of bagged, carefully stored wardrobe pieces, all fully accessorized and most with their original tags.

Since the guests for the birthday bash had been encouraged to wear period clothing, Aunt Mae had insisted on piling all of the outfits she'd bought during the forties and fifties on her bed. One by one, she'd tried them on, postured in front of the mirror, then insisted that Dana mark any alterations needed with straight pins.

Aunt Mae's figure was still lithe and slim—a fact aided by the full-length girdle she invariably wore. But to her dismay, the years had wreaked their havoc in another, more subtle way. She'd shrunk.

So for hours, Dana had sat cross-legged on the floor, making new hemlines. She vaguely remembered sending for Sean before heading upstairs, but she'd seen no sign of him yet. He hadn't bothered to come and create a diversion so that she could find some logical way of abandoning her current task.

A knock at the main door was all the encouragement Dana needed to jump to her feet and hurry into the next room. Rolling her head to ease the kink in her neck, she found Aunt June on the other side.

"There you are, dear. We've begun to decorate the rec hall, but we need your help. Yours and your young man's."

Dana felt a twinge of unease, wondering what Sean had been doing the past few hours on his own.

"Aunt Mae and I—"

"Yes, yes, we know—and she'll be angry that I've come to steal you away," June interrupted. "But we've run out of bunting and streamers. There are more of them in the storage room downstairs. Sean has agreed to bring them up, but he needs you to show him where they are. Once you get into the basement, those stairs down to the boiler room are so creaky, we knew you'd best lead the way. I don't dare send Martha Peabody. Not with that new hip."

"Sure, Aunt June." Dana gestured to the room behind her. "Aunt Mae is about done having me change her hems. She can't decide what to wear tonight."

"Piffle. She didn't have to monopolize you. I'm sure we could have found some taller shoes for her to wear." Aunt June tugged at the brocade vest of the hand-painted caftan she'd chosen to wear that day.

"Never you mind her. *I'll* see to it that she chooses a dress. Then we'll fix one hem. One."

June strode determinedly in the direction of the bedroom, and since Dana didn't want to be forced into the role of referee for the fireworks sure to follow, she slipped into the hall.

There, at the far end, waited Sean O'Malley and Rick Bermen, his camera aimed.

Automatically, she plastered a smile on her face, one she hoped looked airy and natural. "Rick, why don't you take a break?"

"You're sure?"

"Yes. Go get something to eat. We're just heading to the storeroom, so I bet there won't be anything newsworthy with that."

"Fine with me." He swung the camera to his side and disappeared down the stairs.

Dana felt her whole body relax—then grow tense again when she looked Sean's way. She hesitated, swallowing automatically against the tightness that had crept into her throat. He was so tall, so lean, so infinitely male. It alarmed Dana how much she was affected by his nearness. She'd been around beautiful men before. She'd experienced a flutter of attraction to them. But with Sean, it was different. The electricity crackling between them was immediate, heightened by the fact that they'd spent the night alone together.

All alone.

Dana hadn't slept. Sleep had been impossible, knowing he was only a few feet away from her. Wearing little more than briefs. Breathing in and out. In and out. Even the wind rattling the windows hadn't been able to disguise the sounds. Dana had tried folding a pillow over her ears, to no avail. This man had invaded more than her private space. He'd invaded her mind, her will.

As she approached, he straightened from where he'd propped his shoulders against the wall.

"Why didn't you come in with Aunt June?"

His eyes were dark and brooding. "I didn't think it wise to confront Mae any sooner than I had to."

"Oh."

Dana pushed the button for the elevator, curiously loath to meet Sean's gaze again, wondering what she would find there this morning—anger, frustration? Or perhaps even an awareness caused by intimate quarters?

"How was your sleep?" The moment the words were uttered, she wished she could retract them.

"Oh, fine." There was a layer of sarcasm to the reply. "I especially appreciated being awakened by the faint whir of a television camera."

She knew he meant to shame her, but she wasn't about to surrender so quickly.

"I paid for the privilege, remember?"

"You could have warned me."

"Why? You knew I meant to film you this week."

"Yes, but I didn't know you meant to catch me with my clothes off."

The very idea was enough to make her shiver.

"Oh, please," she griped, stabbing the elevator button again. Why was that thing always so blasted slow? Aunt June had told her the contraption had been completely overhauled several months ago, but there had been no evidence of any sort of improvement since the last time Dana had visited. "The way you keep harping on the camera crew, a person would think you have something to hide."

She got no immediate answer, which caused her to peer at him with narrowed eyes. But Sean gave nothing away. Nothing at all. Which merely convinced her all the more that he must have something to hide. Something delicious. Secretive. Intriguing.

"What's the matter, O'Malley? Are you afraid of what I might find out about you?"

He glared at her at the same time the antique elevator ground to a stop. He opened the cage doors and motioned for her to enter.

"After you."

Dana stepped backward into the car, studying every glimpse of emotion that flitted across his face as he closed the gates and asked, "Which floor?"

"Basement."

He poked the appropriate button.

"Are you going to answer my question?" she asked after a moment of silence.

Sean became completely absorbed with the indicator arrow, watching it flicker and descend with evident fascination. "Which question is that?"

"What are you afraid I might find?"

He sighed. "My life is an open book."

"Oh, really?"

"Yes."

She reached around him to punch Stop. The elevator shuddered and grew still.

"Why did you do that?" His question was uttered with the tried patience of an adult handling a recalcitrant child.

"I want an interview from you. On tape."

"No."

He pushed B.

She pushed Stop.

The elevator whined in protest.

"Why not? You said your life was an open book. Prove it."

He punched B again. "I don't have to."

She poked Stop. "What if I tell you I'll demand an interview as part of your week's service?"

A slow anger smoldered in his eyes, but he merely said, "You can do whatever you like, but you won't get any satisfactory answers from me."

When he would have started the elevator again, she grasped his wrist.

"Why are you so set against an interview?"

"I like my privacy."

"My public wants to know more about you."

"So?"

"Doesn't that make you feel the least bit guilty?"

"No."

The word was uttered so bluntly, so implacably, that she knew she wouldn't be getting any cooperation from his end. Not yet. But she had several days—and nights—to work on changing his attitude. By the end of their week together, she expected a totally different response to her request.

"Fine," she uttered blithely. "Do whatever you want."

This time, she was the one to punch B.

There was an ominous shiver, a distant whine. Then nothing.

Scowling, she held the button more firmly. The panel didn't even register her request.

"Now look what you've done," she muttered.

"Me?" Sean leaned against the far wall, his hands resting casually on the railing. "You were the last person to touch it."

"Yes, but if you hadn't been so stubborn about my request—"

His low growl cut off the rest of what she'd been about to say. Moving her to one side as if she were a wayward fly, he pressed the B button for several seconds, then released it.

Not by so much as a moan did the elevator make any sign that the command had been received.

"I already did that," Dana said crossly.

He didn't reply. He was looking upward.

Dana followed his gaze, seeing the trapdoor that led to the upper pulleys and gears.

In one lithe movement, Sean was stepping onto the railings and pushing at the trapdoor.

"Damn. It's been painted or welded shut."

"Probably during its restoration."

"Restoration?" he asked in disbelief.

She could only shrug.

He jumped to the floor, causing the car to shake. Dana gasped, sure that they would plummet to the basement. But the cable held fast.

"There should be a phone in this thing," Sean grumbled.

"As you can see, there isn't."

Because they'd stopped between floors, through the doors only a sliver of light was visible from below—where the ceiling of the first floor would be. Sean knelt, trying to peer through the slit.

"Hello? Hello!"

There was no reply.

"Almost everyone will be in the dining hall by now. It's lunch time. Meals are always an event at Greycliff."

Sighing, Sean sat on the floor, resting his back against the wall and bending his knees. Dana couldn't help noticing the way he folded his arms, drawing attention to the relaxed posture of his hands.

Such strong hands.

Beautiful hands.

Warm hands.

"I guess we'll have to wait until someone tries to use the elevator," Sean said.

She wrenched her thoughts into line with some difficulty. "Yes."

"In the meantime, it looks like we're stuck where we are."

In a stalled elevator.

She and Sean O'Malley.

Dana's lungs seemed to constrict. The air around her became hot and still and resonant with a crackling energy.

She considered sitting on the floor herself—if only to get her bearings—but was afraid that in the cramped confines their limbs would touch. Intertwine.

"How was your morning?" she asked quickly, needing to break the silence.

"Your aunt June proposed sculpting me."

"Nude?" she asked, her voice choked.

"Yes."

Her pulse became a little more rapid. In her mind's eye, she could see such a statue, could see each masculine curve and indentation. After all, hadn't she spent most of the previous night studying him in the weak light thrown into the room by the bathroom door they'd left ajar?

"Well, at least you escaped Aunt April."

"Like hell. She fleeced me out of fifty bucks."

Dana frowned. "Didn't I tell you not to play bridge with her?"

"It was poker."

"Oh. Then I suppose I'll have to see about reimbursing you."

"Add it to your charity tab."

"You mean you won't demand a check from me today?"

"No." In the dim light, his gaze seemed especially mocking. "Somehow, I have a feeling we'll be bargaining like this again soon."

She made a humph of disbelief, but it wasn't very convincing. "We'll see," she drawled.

Then there was nothing to say. Nothing to break the silence that settled around them, heavy and infinitely dangerous.

Dana's heart gave an odd thump. She tried to ignore the fact that the elevator was small, their surroundings incredibly quiet. She sought to keep her mind on something neutral—the grillwork, the tile work—*anything* other than the faint scent of a masculine cologne, the thick waves of Sean's hair. His broad shoulders. The hands of a surgeon.

"Tell me about yourself, Sean," she blurted, hoping that by putting herself into a professional mode, she could forget about the way he was sprawled at her feet.

"Isn't it a little early for an interview? Or do you have a hidden camera hidden in a button somewhere?"

"Very funny."

"I wouldn't put it past you."

"Then you don't know me very well."

"No," he responded slowly, "I don't."

He peered at her through narrowed eyes, making her feel vaguely defenseless in her jeans and loose sweater.

"Why don't you enlighten me?"

She fought the urge to tug at her sweater as it dipped a little too low over one shoulder. Fixing him with her sternest frown, she offered, "I'll only participate if you agree to respond in kind."

"Meaning?"

"I get an answer from you for each one I volunteer."

"Then never mind."

She could have stamped her foot in impatience. In her experience, people enjoyed talking about themselves—it was shutting them up that was often the most difficult part. But this man was determined to remain a complete mystery to her.

Without proper ventilation, the air they breathed was growing that much more heated, that much more charged. It hovered over their shoulders. Close. Intimate. Each moment ticked away with the speed of a snail. Through it all, Dana stared resolutely at the control panel, sure that it would suddenly blink to life.

"Tell me something, Dana," Sean said after a few minutes, rising to his feet.

Dana fought the urge to shrink back against the handrail. "What?" She had hoped for the response to be light and unconcerned, but it emerged as little more than a croak.

"Why is it so important that I be your fiancé? Hmm?"

Her fingers curled around the brass bar, wondering why, in such a small space, he'd felt the need to step closer to her?

"I told you—"

"You offered me some poppycock about wanting to foil your aunts' matchmaking attempts."

"That's right."

"Why?"

He was coming closer, ever closer.

"You don't understand my aunts."

"I don't think anyone could."

"Yes, well, that's true enough. But their idea of a perfect mate is very different from my own."

"In what way?"

"My aunts have a...'Leave It to Beaver' mentality when it comes to marriage." She winced, realizing that her cameramen had compared one of her dates to Beaver.

"What is that supposed to mean?"

"It means that they are trying to find someone who is meek, shy, respectable and nice."

"How awful."

She didn't miss the sarcasm.

"It is, actually."

"Why?"

"Because even if I were considering marrying anyone right now—which I'm not—that's not the sort of man I'd ever choose."

He was so close now that she could feel the heat of his thighs burning through her jeans.

"And what sort *would* you choose?"

She licked her lips, knowing immediately that it was a mistake. Even in the dimness, she could see his gaze drop to her lips.

"I would wish for someone who wasn't so...settled."

"Meaning?"

"I'd like someone who enjoys a good adventure."

"Have you found anyone like that?"

His head was lowering, and she found herself looking at his mouth, at the way his lips had parted ever so subtly.

"No. I haven't been looking."

"Why not?"

Her head tipped of its own volition. "I've been building a career."

"Has that been enough to satisfy you?"

The words took on a totally different connotation as they were processed in her brain.

"What?" she asked weakly.

"Are you satisfied, Dana? Truly satisfied."

She shuddered when his hand circled her ribs, then roamed up, up, up, until his thumb grazed the underside of her breast.

"I've told myself to leave you alone," he rasped close to her ear. "But damn it all to hell. I can't keep my hands off you."

Dana gasped, automatically reaching out to push him away, but growing still as her palms became welded to the strength of his chest, to the muscles molded ever so softly by his shirt.

Then there were no words. Sean was cupping her breast, and she could only moan, a lightning-hot passion streaking through her body. The reaction was so immediate, so stunning, so familiar, that she gasped.

But even that sound was muted when his lips closed over hers. Then there was no time for thought, no time for control. Dana willingly surrendered to the sweetness, the inexplicable pleasure. Her own mouth slanted, parted, becoming hungry. Her hands dragged his shirt free from his jeans and slid underneath to stroke the corrugated muscles of his stomach. Dear heaven above, she'd never known a man could feel like this, hard, firm and slick with a fine layer of perspiration.

A moan gathered deep in her throat. Her exploration continued up, up his body to his chest, to the nipples that were hard and straining. Just like her own.

She fought to get closer, one of her thighs twining between his, but it wasn't enough. Not nearly enough. When Sean lifted her, supporting her on the brass railing, she wrapped her thighs around his waist, needing to grind against him.

"We can't do this," Sean rasped as he dragged his lips away.

She groaned in protest.

"Not in an elevator."

The words—as well as the promise they held—sank slowly into her brain. Blinking, she stared up at him in amazement, wondering if she'd heard him correctly.

"I want to touch you," he whispered against her cheek.

"Yes."

"But I want to do so much more than that."

Her eyes closed, and she dug her fingers into his waist, sensing how difficult it had been for him to make such an admission.

"I'm a private man, Dana. I don't like having people pry into my affairs. You're the last person in the world I should let into my life."

She nuzzled his neck. "Don't think about that now."

When she would have kissed him, he held himself away.

"I'm not someone who takes lovemaking lightly."

She knew that. She'd known that long before he'd actually said the words.

One of her fingers stroked his lips. "Neither am I."

Before he could respond, there was a jarring sensation, a whirring. The lights on the panel lit up at once, and the car shuddered to the first floor.

It was Sean who had the presence of mind to step away and open the gates. Dana used that time to assume a casual pose, but when her aunts appeared in front of her, she decided she shouldn't have bothered.

April flicked Sean's collar with her finger, exposing a streak of Passionate Pomegranate lipstick. "Really, Dana," she chided. "Not the elevator again."

Dana didn't know how to respond to that.

"Do you really think this sort of behavior will get you to the basement to collect our streamers?"

For the first time in her life, Dana took a defensive stand. "How else were we supposed to pass the time?"

April took a drag of her cigar. Then, without a word, she turned and left.

June and Mae, however, were not so easily dismissed.

"We really need those decorations, Dana," June reminded her.

"Yes, I know." She quickly smoothed her sweater and ran a hand over her hair. "We, uh... That is the elevator..."

"Sorry, Aunt June," Sean inserted smoothly. "We'll get them right away." He winked. "Maybe it was for the best. This way, we might be able to keep our minds on the task and off each other.''

June blushed.

Mae gasped in horror.

"However, I think you'll understand if we take the stairs the rest of the way down to the basement.''

But as they disappeared around the corner, Dana didn't miss Aunt Mae's parting comment.

"Cad.''

Chapter Seven

"Well? How do I look?" Sean asked.

Dana glanced up from the felt beret she'd been pinning to her upswept hair to find Sean in the doorway to the bathroom. Turning, she noted the way he'd braced one hand carelessly over his head, causing the jacket of his zoot suit to part and reveal a beautifully tailored shirt and a pair of pleated pants. A watch chain dropped from his belt loop, nearly to his knees, then back to his trouser pocket. His hair had been slicked back with Brylcreem, further emphasizing his rugged features and dark coloring.

"It, uh . . . fine. You look fine."

Dana had always considered the word *fine* to be an inadequate description—and this was no exception. If Ramone C. Peruga had looked anything like this, Dana could understand how her aunts had lost their hearts to the man.

"Will the film crew be tagging along?" Sean asked as he straightened.

"Yes."

She prepared for another salvo of verbal fireworks, but it didn't come. Sean merely nodded and made his way to the dresser, causing her eyes to narrow.

He was being agreeable.

He must be up to something.

"This came for you while you were in the shower." He held up a clear plastic container to reveal a pale pink corsage. "I'll help you put it on."

Dana was perfectly capable of doing such a thing herself, but she didn't protest. Not when it might give Sean the idea that she was reluctant to have him touch her so soon after their encounter in the elevator. She couldn't allow him to know such a thing. To know that their embrace in the elevator had shaken her to the core.

Standing as still as possible, she allowed his fingers to wriggle beneath the slick rayon fabric of the dress she'd borrowed from Aunt Mae. She remained still and quiet as he brushed the top of her breast and fastened the pin.

"There you are."

"Thank you."

"I've been wondering something. How do you plan to explain the fact that you have me masquerading as your fiancé to your oh-so-curious public?"

Dana had wondered when he would bother to ask such a question. "The piece will be edited to remove any such references."

"Aha."

"All we plan to show the public in our feature is the idea of creative dating in the nineties. That and your interview as a local sex symbol."

He didn't comment, and her unease only increased. He *was* up to something. She *knew* he was up to something.

"You seem very agreeable this evening." Her suspicion was not completely disguised.

"I love movies."

"We're seeing three hours of newsreels and short films made by my aunts."

"So?"

"So, there's a reason they didn't make the transition to Hollywood as successfully as they would have liked."

He shrugged with complete indifference. "Whatever."

"Be warned, there will be a quiz afterward."

"A quiz?"

"My aunts will drill you for your impressions of their work."

"Ah."

A knock at the door signaled the arrival of the camera crew.

"Ready?" Dana asked, suddenly wishing that they could spend this evening alone, without her co-workers.

Sean didn't answer. He merely opened the door and gestured for her to precede him outside.

As soon as they'd fallen into place in the hall, Rick and Adam took position behind them.

"Put your arm around me," Dana whispered.

"Won't your public be shocked?"

"Why would they?" She grasped his arm and wound it around her waist herself.

"From what I've always seen, you have a reputation for being a bit of an ice princess."

Up to this moment, Sean had been watching her carefully, waiting for some kind of reaction, but when it came, it was far from what he'd expected.

Her eyes sparkled in delight, and she grinned. "Really?"

"That pleases you?"

"Why not? It adds more credence to my job as a professional if I don't come across looking like I'm on the make."

On the make. He hadn't heard that phrase in years. Sean's lips twitched in unwilling amusement. He kept trying to reestablish his anger at the way this woman had thrust him into a very compromising position. But just when he felt he had his emotions in line, Dana said something totally unexpected.

She was a curious woman. An odd mixture of competency, professionalism, toughness...

And vulnerability.

It was her aunts who brought out that particular trait. If it weren't for them, Sean might never have had a glimpse of what Dana must have been like when she was younger and a little less sure of herself. And even though he might not approve of her methods for bringing him here, for trying to force some sort of interview out of him, he was beginning to understand why she'd done it. Being a blood relation to April, Mae and June Flowers would have been enough to drive anyone to drink.

As if on cue, he and Dana turned the last corner to find the triplets waiting for them by the entrance to the recreational room.

April was sporting her customary cigarillo, but she'd changed into a shantung sheath—beige. Mae was decked out in a beaded evening gown with a huge feather boa that she'd wrapped around her face so that only the black sunglasses peered out at him. Then there was June, dear June, looking like Greycliff's answer to Barbara Cartland with her hair, her gown, her jewelry and her dog all dyed a soft, glowing pink.

"Sean, darling!" June called, but when she would have rushed forward to greet them, April snagged her wrist.

"Leave them alone, June."

"But—"

"We've got other guests to greet."

"I only want to—"

"You want to conduct some sort of... artistic inspection—one that doesn't involve your eyes. Leave them alone."

June pouted.

Babbette growled.

April glared at the animal, muttering, "Quiet."

Sean waited a half step away as Dana dutifully kissed each powdered cheek. To his relief, a tinny sort of music began to waft into the hall from the darkened room.

"Hurry, hurry!" June exclaimed, Babbette yapping in accompaniment. "You mustn't miss the first newsreel. It's of our trip to London."

Dana took that opportunity to cut her greetings short and drag Sean into the recreation room. "I'll get us a seat up there." She pointed to a nearly empty row of chairs near the screen. "You get the doughnuts and lemonade."

"Doughnuts?"

"They wanted to give an air of a U.S.O. canteen."

"I thought such places served doughnuts and coffee."

"Most did, but Aunt Mae loves lemonade. It's her favorite. Besides, Aunt April didn't want to deal with the caffeine issue."

"What caffeine issue?"

"She's sure some of the men at the village get quite... frisky when they've been indulging in the stuff."

Sean stood where he was, watching Dana make her way to the folding chairs, noting the way the rayon of her dress clung to her hips and swayed around her shapely legs.

If he didn't know better, he would think she'd stepped from a post-war scrapbook with her hat, her hair in sausage rolls, the dress. And those hose. Sean found himself riveted to the seams stretching up her calves, and he couldn't help but wonder if she were wearing a garter belt.

A warmth settled low in his stomach. Why had women ever abandoned such a fashion as seamed hosiery and garter belts? He found them both fascinating. Completely and utterly fascinating.

Arousing.

At least on Dana.

Turning, Sean made his way through the wheelchairs and walkers parked at the back of the room. Despite the weather, there was quite a crowd in attendance. It made him smile to see the little clumps of elderly women with their fresh hairdos and bright red lipstick. Some of the gentlemen had worn their uniforms—their jackets either hanging from their frames or refusing to button completely in the front. It was obvious from the excitement in the air that this was an event to be cherished. A chance to revel in the glory days of their youth.

Sean joined the queue of people waiting for refreshments at a table decorated with red, white and blue bunting. Rows of paper cups full of lemonade and plates of fresh doughnuts awaited selection from the guests. One of the women he recognized as part of the poker group from earlier in the day was distributing napkins and overseeing the serving of refreshments. When she saw him waiting in line, she offered him a bold wink mouthing, "Tomorrow." Somehow, Sean knew he would be back at the gaming tables with April and the rest of her card sharks no matter what he might say to the contrary.

Sean was nearly the head of the line when he felt a slight pressure at his sleeve. Looking down, he was shocked to find Mae Flowers peering at him above the rims of her sunglasses. Her eyes were incredibly blue and bright, even in the dim light.

"I know what you're doing," she accused.

"Doing?"

"You're trying to make me jealous."

Now, how in hell was he supposed to respond to that?

"I won't have it, you know. Not with my own niece."

"I assure you, I—"

"Hush!" she interrupted. "I don't want to hear your lies. I know what you want, and it won't work. I won't come back to you, Ramone."

When he would have spoken, she placed a finger over his lips.

"No. Don't talk. Don't try to change my mind. I've made a life without you, Ramone. You need to accept it."

Then she was gone in a rustle of beads, a single feather escaping from her boa and floating to the floor behind her.

Sean shook his head in disbelief. If he wasn't mistaken, he'd just been dumped. By a woman over twice his age.

Shrugging, he made his way back to Dana, handing her a cup and one of the doughnuts.

"What did she say?"

He didn't question how she'd known her aunt Mae had spoken to him. Although he'd never seen Dana turn to look at him, he'd felt her gaze now and again.

"She dumped me."

"What?"

"She dumped me. She's quite upset that I've been using you as a pawn to make her jealous, and she feels that I should know she's made a life for herself without me. She thinks I should move on."

Dana stared at him as if he were speaking a foreign language, then she chuckled. "Aunt Mae is a character," she muttered softly to herself.

The lights began to dim. A black-and-white countdown appeared on the screen in the front of the room.

"I couldn't agree more," Sean responded.

"Shh."

The two of them lapsed into silence as the first newsreel began. Sean sipped at his lemonade, then took a bite of his doughnut. Spudnuts. Just like those his grandmother used to make, he thought, absorbing the old, familiar tastes and textures. He'd only been fourteen when the last of his grandparents had passed away, and he often missed them. Dana was lucky to have three doting aunts who—

The thought screeched to a halt in his brain.

Lucky?

Lucky?

But even as he questioned such a choice of words, he couldn't deny it. Yes, she was lucky to have three kooky women who loved her so completely. Despite their overprotectiveness, they doted on her. It would be nice to have that sort of influence in a person's life.

A tightness eased into Sean's chest, and he tried to push it away, but try as he might, he couldn't help thinking about his own family. His mother had been gone long enough for her passing to ease into a dull ache, but his father...

Sean still couldn't resign himself to the fact that Robert O'Malley was lying in a hospital bed in a coma. A coma that had lingered for nearly a year and had thrown their family into turmoil. Sean's father had been so sure of his own immortality that he hadn't bothered to update his will from one made twelve years ago. One that named a distant aunt and uncle as guardians to his children. It was that particular point Sean was trying to overturn. Something he couldn't do unless he could prove that his three youngest sisters would have a completely stable home under his care.

He sighed, worrying, wondering how Mary-Kate was doing at home. She'd been left in charge of the family in his absence, but Sean knew she was too young to be responsible for so much. Especially considering the turmoil being caused by the custody battle.

The tension in his chest increased, and he tried to douse it with a swig of lemonade, but it didn't really help.

"Is something wrong?"

Dana laid a hand on his thigh, and he found himself staring at it, at the slender fingers and shapely nails. The warmth of her skin seeped through his clothing.

"No, nothing's wrong," he murmured, twining his own fingers between hers, knowing that there would be no use in explaining. He was her temporary fiancé. Her auctioned escort. In less than a week, they would part company and rejoin the real world.

One where the scent of face powder and hair cream was a thing of the past.

"DANA? DANA!"

Sean awakened from a groggy sleep to hear a pounding on the outer door of the honeymoon suite. Recognizing June's voice, he drew the pillow over his head, hoping against hope that whatever the woman wanted, it didn't involve him and a bucket of plaster of paris.

Vainly, he fought to regain some shred of sleep. He'd spent most of the night lying awake, alternately staring at the ceiling...and Dana.

He wondered if she knew that she curled into a little ball as she slumbered, that she tucked her hands under her cheek like a child. He wondered if she knew that every once in a while, she would mumble something. And that at least once, he'd been sure he'd caught his own name.

Had she been dreaming of him?

A finger touched his shoulder, and he jumped, pushing the pillow away. Dana bent over him, her hair swinging softly about her face, her skin clear and pink and bare of all makeup.

"Sean, the storm has grown even worse."

It took a moment for his brain to assimilate the information. He couldn't seem to tear his eyes away from the too-large T-shirt she'd been wearing to bed the past couple of evenings. He was sure she'd chosen the garment as an attempt to dissuade him from lascivious thoughts. That, combined with a pair of old gym shorts and tube socks, should have been off-putting to any man.

Any man but Sean.

He found the outfit completely charming. It was far from businesslike, far from sophisticated, making her appear less of a newswoman and more of the girl next door.

She poked him again.

"Are you awake?"

"Mmm." The grunt was all he could manage, especially when confronted with the fact that her breasts were swaying softly against her T-shirt.

"There's been a power outage."

He dragged his attention to the room itself, and then to the windows beyond. Although the drapes were all but closed, he saw enough of the weather to deduce that a full-scale blizzard was raging outside. And as the gist of Dana's announcement sank into his consciousness, he grew aware of the chill to the air.

"My aunts are all in a dither because the heat has failed. They wondered if you would be willing to go out to the power shack and see if you can get the generator to work."

"They want me to go out in that?" he asked, gesturing to the whirling snow on the other side of the glass.

"Either we try to help, or over a hundred retired residents are going to freeze to death."

We.

"You're going, too?"

She straightened, obviously becoming aware of the way she hovered over him.

"I'll have to. You won't know where the place is, otherwise. Not with such limited visibility."

He didn't argue. He didn't want to argue.

"Fine."

His quick capitulation must have surprised her because her eyes narrowed. "Really?"

"Sure."

Her fingers toyed nervously with the hem of her shorts, drawing his attention to her legs, those long, lean legs.

"You'd better get dressed, Dana," he said slowly, then met her gaze. "Otherwise..."

She didn't wait for his response. Whirling, she rushed into the bathroom and slammed the door.

He chuckled, throwing back the covers and standing. He was reaching for his jeans when the bathroom door whipped open again.

"Wait a minute, I have to—"

She froze.

He froze.

Even the cool temperature of the bedroom couldn't disguise the heat that sprang between them.

Sean felt the way her gaze dipped convulsively to the region of his hips, clung for a moment, then bounced up again. The completely spontaneous reaction was enough to cause an answering reflex from his own body.

"Oh."

Her soft exhalation caused a rash of gooseflesh to claim his back.

It was the only sound for some time—as long as Sean didn't count the thumping of his heart in his ears or the rasp of his own breath.

"Get into the bathroom, Dana," he warned, knowing that if he didn't speak, he might not have the ability to do so.

But she didn't move.

Heaven help her, she didn't move.

The jeans slipped from his fingers to the floor, and he took a step. Two. Then she must have realized that if he took one more, there would be no turning back. Not now. Not ever.

Whirling, she closed the door behind her, and he stood immobile, glad that she had run from the temptation—yet wishing that she hadn't. That she'd stayed. Melted into his arms.

Breathing deeply, he bent, slipping into his trousers. After dragging the rest of his clothes over his body, he strode into the darkened hall.

He would wait for her at the front door.

Where it was safe.

DANA HEARD HIM go and wilted against the wooden panels, staring into the mirror over the sink. Incredibly, she supposed the woman who stared back at her was really Dana Shaw, but she wasn't so sure. She'd never witnessed that feverish light in her own eyes before.

"Damn," she whispered to herself, sinking onto the floor and burying her face in her bent knees. This couldn't be happening. She'd always prided herself on being completely professional. Never in her career had she allowed herself to become emotionally involved with one of her subjects. It was wrong. It went against every professional and ethical code she had ever set for herself.

But the silent castigation had little effect on the way her blood ran through her veins at a riotous pace.

When she'd been young, her aunts had made it a habit to visit a movie theater at least once a week. Since their tastes veered toward romantic comedies and love stories, Dana had been given a steady diet of such fare. She'd been so sure she knew just what love felt like.

Unfortunately, all of the experiences she'd ever had with men had fallen short of such lofty ideals. She'd decided that building a relationship wasn't really worth the time or the effort.

Until now.

She pressed her hands to her hot cheeks.

How could he make her feel so alive?

The last thought stuck in her brain, refusing to be budged. But she supposed it was true. She might have a job that others envied, and she might lead a life of independence and excitement. But lately, there had been times—times she hadn't admitted even to herself—when she'd felt as if something was missing.

No, not something. Someone.

Her hands dropped, and she rested her head against the door, closing her eyes. It was one thing to admit that she might be lacking an elemental piece to her overall happiness. But wasn't it going too far to expect that final bit of the puzzle to be found in Sean O'Malley? Calendar man? Volunteer fireman?

Wasn't that a bit much to ask of anyone she'd known for such a short time?

Sighing, she pushed herself to her feet, ignoring her own reflection in the mirror. She wouldn't think about it right now—a very Scarlett O'Hara-like response and one that was totally unlike her. But she didn't really care. After all, there was only so much worrying a person's nerves could take in one day.

Walking out and finding Sean O'Malley wearing nothing but his briefs would have been enough of a shock to anyone's system.

Not that there had been anything wrong with what she'd seen, she amended quickly. She'd seen dozens of men in bathing suits much briefer than anything she'd witnessed today.

Nevertheless, she couldn't remember the last time she'd seen a man fill them up in quite the same way.

Stop it! Get a hold of yourself!

Jerking her thoughts into line, she hurried into the bedroom to put on her clothes. Even so, she couldn't prevent the way she automatically reached for the prettiest set of lingerie she'd brought with her to Greycliff Village.

Chapter Eight

Less than fifteen minutes later, Dana was hurrying down the corridor to the front door, which was illuminated by emergency lights. She'd nearly made her way to the bottom when Aunt Mae appeared in front of her, forcing her headlong pace to ease.

"Dana, I have someone I'd like you to meet."

The words were enough to send a very real shiver of fear through her heart.

Mae stepped aside to reveal a man who was a good half foot shorter than Mae with the lithe form of a jockey.

When he saw Dana, he flushed to the roots of his hair and pushed at the glasses slipping down his nose.

"This is Mort."

Mort the mortician.

Dana remembered Rick and Adam's prediction that one of her aunts would line her up with this man. She fought the hopelessness swelling in her bosom. Why couldn't her aunts see that even though the men they sent her way were quite charming, they weren't Dana's type. She wanted someone more like...

When her gaze lifted, connecting with Sean's across the hall, she couldn't help the way her mind finished, *like him.*

"Dana?"

At her aunt's prompting, she shook Mort's hand.

"I hope I'll be seeing you at the ball, Dana."

"Yes, yes, I suppose you will," she replied absently.

"I'd be honored if you'd save me a waltz."

A waltz. She'd been there when Sean had been taught the finer points of the dance.

"I suppose I could if my fiancé doesn't mind."

At the word *fiancé,* Mort's features clouded.

"You're going to be married?"

"Yes." She met Sean's gaze again, wishing she didn't have to lie. "Yes, I am."

"I see."

It was obvious that she had ruined his entire day.

"Congratulations."

The tone of voice Mort employed would have been more in keeping with "Eat dirt and die," but Dana didn't comment.

Without another word, Mort turned and made his way toward one of the employee doors, the hem of his coat flapping behind him.

"You could have been a little nicer, Dana," Mae chided.

Dana sighed. "Aunt Mae, I thought you realized that I was going to marry Sean."

Mae snorted. "It will never happen," she intoned fatefully, then made her own hasty retreat, leaving Dana to wish that her aunt hadn't sounded quite so prophetic.

"Ready?" Sean asked.

"Sure."

She gave the man a wide berth as she walked out the front door.

Once she stepped outside, she peered under the eaves in disbelief. To be honest, she'd been so busy lately that she hadn't bothered to check on things other than a quick peek out the window now and again. To her horror, she saw that over a foot of drifting snow had gathered beneath the portico and at least three times that had collected on the ground.

Sean came up behind her, tugging on his gloves.

"Quite a storm, isn't it?"

She couldn't speak, though her silence was not from her surprise at the effects of the weather. No, it was the way the hairs at the back of her neck rose and her skin began to tingle.

"Your coat," she murmured. "How did you get it back?"

"Aunt June."

"You're lucky she didn't steal it."

"She did. One of April's bridge cronies told me where to find it."

Dana felt a heat creeping up her neck as if she were responsible for the theft. "I'm sorry, I—"

"It wasn't your fault. Don't worry about it. June was very gracious when she gave it back."

"How gracious?" Dana asked suspiciously.

"*Very* gracious."

When he didn't elaborate, she decided she didn't want to know the details. Instead, she peered at the snow slanting toward them with ferocious power.

"We'll never get to the gardener's shed this way. We're going to need snowshoes or something."

"I've already taken care of that." Sean pointed to a dark shape that was barely visible through the whipping flakes. "Your aunt April suggested that we take Madison's snowmobile."

"Madison's?" she echoed in disbelief, remembering the decrepit old man who served as Aunt April's butler of sorts. He had to be ninety if he was a day. "The machine belongs to *Madison?*"

Sean shrugged. "Go figure." He studied her closely. "Are you ready?"

She nodded, but when she would have stepped away, he stopped her with a light touch on her neck. Before she knew what he meant to do, he tied her scarf a little more tightly around her throat and pulled her hat over the tips of her ears.

"We can't have you getting frostbite."

The words were so soft, she wouldn't have thought he'd said them at all if she hadn't seen them being formed on his lips.

She didn't know how to respond. But before such a fact could become obvious, he put a palm at her waist and led her to the snowmobile.

He straddled the broad black seat, turned the key and coaxed the engine into life. After he'd revved it a couple of times, he held out a hand. A broad hand sheathed in a black leather glove.

Steadying herself against his shoulder, she settled behind him, all too aware of the way his broad shoulders cut some of the wind, preventing it from chafing her cheeks.

"Keep your arms around my waist," he shouted.

She nodded, doing as she was told, conscious of the rock-hard muscles she gripped.

"Where do we go?" he asked after revving the snowmobile again.

"Down the hill and to the left. The gardener's shack is located just east of the bridge."

He nodded. "Hold on."

There was a roar, and the snowmobile shot forward. Afraid she might be dumped into the powder, Dana burrowed her cheek against his back and dug her fingers into the fabric of his coat.

It took over fifteen minutes for them to make their way down the slope—a distance that could have been covered in a third the time in any other weather. They even made a mistake, overshooting the building by a hundred yards once because of the poor visibility, but soon they were riding up to the main door.

Sean killed the engine. "Get inside, Dana."

She didn't wait for another invitation, but hopped from the machine and hurried to the old-fashioned door with its multipaned window. Jiggling the knob and jamming her shoulder against the wood, she finally persuaded it to swing open.

Seconds later, Sean followed, shutting them inside.

"Whew!" He dragged his hat free and shook his head to dislodge the snow frozen to the thick strands.

"There should be some lamps and things in here," Dana said, feeling her way over the counter next to the door. Little more than a weak light managed to find its way into the interior. "This building is used more as a storage facility for lawn furniture and summer supplies than anything else. As I recall from the last time I was sent down here to fetch something, there were a dozen citronella lamps about...here!" she finished in delight.

"What about matches?"

She reached into her pocket, removing a lighter. "I came prepared."

"I'm impressed."

"Don't be. I came prepared for Aunt April's cigarettes, not for these lamps." The rasp of the flint preceded a flare of light, and she used the opportunity to pull the lanterns closer. Within seconds, the gardener's hut glowed, a citrusy smell wafting into the air around them.

"Where's the generator?"

She shrugged, looking around her, but mounds of wicker lawn furniture and bright gingham cushions obscured most of the shelves. "Is that it?"

When she pointed to a round, towerlike structure, Sean frowned. But the expression was quickly replaced by a slow smile.

"I'll be damned." He knelt beside the contraption, opening a tiny door at the base. "Give me your lighter."

She set it in his outstretched palm, wondering how he planned to fix a generator with a cigarette lighter. But when he pressed a button, touched the tip of the flame to something in the center and a coil of dancing fire ignited, she made a soft "Ooh" of pleasure.

"A space heater," she breathed.

"It's probably kept here for just such an occasion. According to the gauge, there's nearly a full tank of propane."

Dana moved closer, holding her hands out to the warmth already beginning to radiate from the contraption. "Thank goodness. I was afraid we'd freeze to death trying to find that blasted generator."

Sean was already moving a couch aside and another chaise. At his soft "Aha," Dana knew they'd hit pay dirt.

"Your aunt said there would be some tools in the cupboard by the door. Would you see what you can find?"

It wasn't difficult to locate the old-fashioned toolbox beneath the workbench, and she hefted it over to the spot where Sean had dropped onto the floor.

Taking a seat on the end of the chaise beside him, she said, "I can hand you the tools if you'd like."

"Do you know what a ratchet is?"

"I've been a single woman living on my own for nearly ten years. Not only do I know what a ratchet is, I can grout my own shower and rewire electrical appliances."

He offered her a low whistle. "A woman of the nineties."

"The nineties or any other generation. My aunts were adamant about my receiving a complete education—including basic auto maintenance and budgeting. They refused to allow me to become a helpless female."

"I hope my own sisters will be as capable when they're off on their own. Sometimes, I'm not so sure."

Dana became still, realizing that Sean was volunteering personal information—a rare occurrence indeed.

"Are they very young?"

"Some are, some aren't." He was stretching out on the floor on his back and squinting at the engine positioned near his head. "Carol is the oldest. She just turned twenty and is a sophomore at the University of Utah. I'll be glad once she finishes moving into this little bungalow she's sharing with some friends for the rest of the year. That's about the only way I'll get my truck back. She's been 'borrowing' it for the better part of a month."

His words might hold a hint of a complaint, but his tone was indulgent.

"The next O'Malley sibling is Mary-Kate. She must be some kind of throwback to the original O'Malleys because she has carrot red hair and a face full of freckles. She's the musician of the family—a freshman at Utah State University in Logan."

"What does she play?"

He grimaced. "The drums."

Dana laughed.

"It was hell when she first started. I finally insulated one of the old chicken coops, hung wallboard and persuaded her to practice out there."

"So she's eighteen? Nineteen?"

"Seventeen. She graduated a year early. All honors."

"I'm impressed."

"So am I," he admitted somewhat sheepishly.

"Ashley is next in line. She's sixteen going on twenty-seven. She has long blond hair, a face like Alice in Wonderland and a gaggle of boys that follows her everywhere she goes."

As he spoke, she mentally ticked off the girls on her fingers. Three down.

"Robin and Jessica are twins, fifteen. They've got it in their head that they want to invent something. It doesn't matter what it is, exactly, as long as it's new and a benefit to mankind."

"That sounds noble."

"Hardly. They've blown up more outbuildings than I'd care to mention. It's probably because of them I joined the volunteer fire department. I was beginning to know everyone on the crew on a first-name basis."

Dana pulled her feet onto the chaise, wrapping her arms around her knees and grinning. "You're exaggerating."

"Not by much. Thank goodness they finished their introduction-to-chemistry class at school. I can only hope that physical science won't give them any ideas."

He was fiddling with a set of wires, so Dana waited until he'd finished before prompting, "That leaves the three youngest O'Malley children."

"The youngest and the most spoiled. Mom's diabetes was a result of the pregnancy with the twins, and she swore she wasn't going to have any more babies."

"What happened?" Dana asked, wondering if that was too personal a question.

"She fell off the wagon. She had a knack with babies, a way of making them happy no matter how cantankerous they could be. She ran a daycare in our house for a few years—as much to provide us with playmates as anything else. But she kept saying it wasn't the same. I suppose because we were older by then, we spoiled the hell out of the last three girls."

"What are their names?"

"Ellen is seven. She's got a thing for dolls—especially baby dolls. I have a feeling that of all of us, she's the most like Mom. Marcia is five, already reading like a pro and more tomboy than little girl. Then there's Deborah. She's four and still at that age where she can be a terror one minute, then flash an angelic smile that makes you feel like a worm for ever yelling at her."

By the time he'd finished, Dana was dumbfounded. What a marvelous family. Sean was so lucky to have grown up with so many fascinating siblings. In a flash, she could see them all ripping into Christmas wrapping or fighting for the bathroom.

"I can't even imagine how wonderful your mother must have been."

At her comment, Sean peered up at her, a strange stillness settling over his frame.

Dana was instantly self-conscious. "Did I say something wrong?" she asked, wondering if all mention of his mother was still too painful.

"No, not at all." His lips twitched. "It's just that most people are quick to condemn her for having so many children, instead of complimenting her for it."

"How long has it been since she died?"

"Nearly two years."

"That must have been very difficult for all of you."

He nodded. "Especially the younger kids."

"And your father...?" she prompted, wondering if she were treading on dangerous ground with her questions, but needing to know. Not for some interview, but for herself.

"He had his accident the following summer."

"So you've been taking care of all those children by yourself?"

"Not by myself. The oldest girls do a lot of the work. In fact, they're much better than I am at bandaging knees and such."

She doubted that very much. There was a fondness to his tone that revealed he loved his little sisters very much.

"It must be difficult being responsible for so many children."

Again, the careless shrug, but there was a tenseness to his shoulders that had not been there before.

"What is it, Sean?"

It was obvious that he didn't mean to confide in her. But after a moment's hesitation, he said, "There have been some problems with the legalities of becoming their guardian."

"What kind of problems?"

"My father never bothered to leave a living will, and one of my aunts wants to take the three youngest girls to live with her. We don't want the family split up."

"Can they do that?"

"If they can prove Ellen, Deborah and Marcia wouldn't be better off where they are."

"Oh."

A silence settled over the hut as Sean returned to his task. Since he didn't seem inclined to say any more, Dana didn't push. She already felt a certain joy at knowing that he had decided to trust her with that much information. She couldn't help thinking that if the public knew even half of what this man was like, they would love him for far more than his body.

"Why did you model for the calendar?"

He glanced at her muttering, "I need a Phillips screwdriver."

She selected the appropriate tool and waited. When he didn't answer, she said, "Well?"

Again, he peered her way. "The truth?"

She nodded.

"We needed a new roof on the firehouse."

"That's very selfless of you."

He grinned. "Not really. By donating the money, I didn't have to spend three days working on it during the middle of July."

Dana wasn't sure if she should believe such an explanation, but she didn't refute it.

"How about you?" Sean asked.

"What about me?"

"Why did you become a news reporter?"

"I like to talk."

He grinned. "I never would have guessed." He was examining the spark plugs.

"And why did you feel it necessary to buy yourself a fiancé?"

Dana rolled her eyes. "You already know the answer to that."

"Not really. Why buy one? You must have had plenty of men who would be willing to volunteer for the part."

She sensed a compliment in there somewhere.

"Why go to an auction and risk hiring a stranger?"

"It was a . . . spontaneous decision. The tickets to the auction were left to my friend and me by a very dear friend who died recently." When she caught Sean's interested gaze, she elaborated. "Dottie was our surrogate mother during our college years when we stayed in her home in the Avenues. She left us the tickets in her will along with a thousand dollars and the instructions to spend the money on something other than bills." Dana toyed with the end of a ratchet. "I convinced my friend to go, knowing I'd find someone I could bring to this event. I thought if I 'bought' an escort, I could prevent any difficulties later on."

"Difficulties?"

"Like thinking that the charade was real."

His eyes grew dark, filled with secrets. "I see. Is there a pair of pliers in there?"

"Mm-hmm."

She took the metal grippers from the box, but as she passed them, the handles slipped from her fingers. Horrified, she watched at they flew through the air, smacking Sean on the left cheekbone.

"Oh, my, gosh." She was down on her knees in an instant, the toolbox clattering across the floor and scattering its contents. "Are you hurt?"

Without thinking, she straddled his waist and leaned down, dragging his own hand away from his eye.

Their gazes met. Locked. The gardener's shack became suddenly small. Intimate. Warm.

"Are you hurt?"

Rather than answering her, he slid his fingers into her hair, cupping the back of her skull.

"Why do you have to be so damn beautiful?" he asked. The question was so unexpected, she couldn't move, couldn't think.

Then there were no words at all as he pulled her resolutely toward him, his lips trailing up her jaw to the corner of her eye, her temple, her hair.

"I've never met anyone in my life so damn beautiful," he whispered against her ear.

Although Dana wasn't sure who moved, their lips met, the caress so gentle, so slow, so leisurely, that her blood began to move thick and molten through her veins. Her fingers spread wide, pressing into the resiliency of his chest.

"We shouldn't be doing this," she whispered when they parted for air.

"No." He was stroking the crease of her spine.

"I don't have room in my life for complications."

"Neither do I."

"I don't have room in my life for a relationship."

"Neither do I."

"We should get up."

"Mm-hmm."

"We should open the window a crack."

"Whatever."

Then they were kissing again, the caress long and slow and deep. Dana melted into his body, reclining over him, her legs twining intimately with his.

He rolled her to her back, planting a string of kisses down her throat to the hollow at the base of her collarbone. With the lightest of pressure, he unzipped her coat and began to unfasten the buttons of her flannel shirt.

"Beautiful," he sighed when she was bared to him, her breasts cupped by a flowered bra edged in black lace. "So very beautiful."

He held her fullness in the hollow of his palm, making her arch against him, a fire igniting in the pit of her belly. Her eyes closed, but even then, she imagined each nuance of his body, the thickness of his hair, the fire of his eyes.

His body rubbed against hers as he moved upward again for a kiss.

"This is going so fast," she whispered. "I've known you only a few days."

"Is that all?"

The words were poetry. *Is that all?*

"I feel like I've known you forever."

Dana could have stopped breathing when she felt the words against the side of her neck. In one brief instant, she realized how lonely her life had been. How completely solitary. Her heart soaked up the sentiments as if she'd been love starved.

"I'm so glad we didn't bring Adam or Rick with us."

The moment the words were said, Dana wished she could snatch them back. The man above her became still, tense. Then he rolled away, bending his knees.

Dana closed her eyes, her hands balling into fists, damning herself for being an idiot.

"I shouldn't have mentioned that." She didn't know what else to say, but even as she tried, she knew the phrase wouldn't be enough.

"You still plan to hold me to the interview?"

"Yes. You must have known that I would. We'll film it early Sunday afternoon."

He sighed, raking his fingers through his hair. "What would it take to stop it?"

"I don't want to stop it."

"I thought I made it clear that I didn't want to do it."

"And I thought I made it clear that I'd paid for the opportunity and I intended to see it through."

He wiped a hand over his face. "So was this all an act? A way to make me more agreeable to the idea?"

He couldn't have hurt her more had he slapped her.

Jumping to her feet, she scrambled to fasten her buttons, but before she could finish, he moved up behind her, holding her arms still.

"I'm sorry, that was a rotten thing to say."

"Yes. It was."

He sighed, and she thought she felt the pressure of his lips against her hair. "You meant to buy my services to keep things from becoming complicated," he murmured. "But they are already very, very complicated."

She couldn't answer, not without revealing that her throat had all but closed, so she nodded.

"It will get worse before it gets better."

Again, her chin dipped.

"But we can't ignore what's happening here."

No. No, they couldn't.

Sighing, he turned her to face him, staring down.

"So we'll take things one day at a time. And if this whole thing blows up in our faces, then at least we've tried."

"Yes." It was the only word she could manage to push past her lips.

Then she was stepping into his arms, holding him, loving him, caressing him.

It was several minutes later before Sean stepped away.

"The generator," he muttered to himself. "We've got to see to the generator first." But as he crossed to the engine, he paused and peered out the window. "I'll be damned. There are lights up there."

"You're kidding."

Dana stepped behind him, peering over his shoulder. Even in the storm, Greycliff was ablaze.

"The power must have come on," she said.

"I suppose it's just as well. The spark plugs in the generator are pretty well useless. I don't think we'll be getting anything out of them."

"Then I suppose we should head back," Dana said with infinite regret.

The words seemed to echo around them. *Head back.* To a shared room. Intimate quarters.

Pretending to be in love.

"I think that would be best," Sean said slowly. "If not, I'll be dragging you down on this floor for good. And it won't be for the purpose of fixing the generator."

Chapter Nine

It took several seconds for Dana to push away the effects of that statement, but at long last, she found the energy to repair her clothing and don her winter gear.

Sean turned off the heater, then before they stepped into the cold, he drew her close, framing her face in his hands. "Are you angry that I suggested going back?"

She shook her head. "Why should I be angry?" She touched his chin with her thumb. "You drew a halt to something that was going too fast, that's all."

But what lay unspoken between the two of them was the fact that neither had really wanted to stop. There were just as many regrets in putting space between them as there would have been had they made love.

"It's going too fast," Sean said again.

But Dana wasn't so sure any more. True, they had only known each other for a few days, but she already felt as if she knew this man in a way she had known no other before. She didn't understand how or why. All she knew was that her heart ached in accompaniment with her body.

He must have sensed her hesitation, because Sean reached for her hand, drawing it between them. Slowly, gently, resolutely, he twined their fingers together—in a way that reminded Dana of how recently their bodies had done much the same thing.

"When we get back," he began, "and your aunts begin to follow us around—" he grinned "—remember what it was like to roll around on the floor of the gardener's shack. Remember that hint of danger, the excitement, the damn-them-all way you felt." He brushed his lips over hers, saying into her mouth. "Then remember me and blush just the way you're blushing now."

She tried to duck her head in embarrassment, wondering why this particular man had the ability to make her feel like an adolescent. She was thirty years old, for heaven's sake. He shouldn't be able to make her knees quake with a single glance.

But he did.

And it was one of the most wonderful feelings she'd experienced in a very long time.

The cold air swirled between them, and Dana was reminded of the fact that they'd paused beneath the eaves.

"Come on," Sean urged.

Swinging his leg over the bench seat of the snow-mobile, he waited for her to take the place behind him.

Dana complied without a word, but this time, as her arms wound about his waist, there was no hesitancy, no tension. She held herself as close to him as she possibly could, burying her head against his back.

"Ready?"

"Yes."

The machine jolted to a start and began racing across the snow, heading up the hill to Greycliff. Dana laughed out loud at the exhilaration of flying from one drift over a dip in the snow, then landing in six inches of powder. Sensing her enjoyment, Sean began to race in and out of the trees—and for a moment, the storm was forgotten. There were only the two of them, the machine and the snow.

It was as he was heading through a stand of oak trees at the bottom of the hill when Dana thought she heard an odd lapse to the rhythm of the engine. A slight hitching. She frowned.

"Sean, is something wrong?"

Almost simultaneously, the engine stalled and died.

She heard Sean swear under his breath and watched the way the muscles in his arms strained as he fought to bring the machine to a stop beneath a stand of trees. Then there was nothing but silence and the eerie whistle of the wind.

"What's wrong?" she asked as Sean fussed with the controls. Only after he'd opened the gas tank and peered inside did he stop.

"It's out of fuel."

Dana peered over his shoulder. "But the gauge says it's half-full."

"The gauge is wrong."

The heavy storm clouds that were gathering had caused a premature darkness to descend around them, and with it came the cold. Dana chafed her hands together, wishing she'd thought to bring something heavier than the knit mittens she wore. Even in the gardener's shack, she could have borrowed some thick work gloves, but she hadn't realized how warm the gardener's shack had grown until this moment as icy tendrils of wind began to burrow under her clothing.

"What are we going to do?" she asked softly.

"We'll have to walk."

"Walk?" she echoed weakly, gazing up the steep slope to the sprawling retirement village beyond. "You're sure?"

"Unless you've got some gasoline hidden in your pocket."

She shook her head—even though there was no real need to do so.

Sean slid feetfirst into the drift beside them, caught his balance, then reached to help her dismount.

"Come on."

There was no sense prolonging the inevitable, she supposed as she took his hand and allowed him to pull her upright.

The mounds of snow were deeper here than they had been nearer to the road and Sean was forced to go ahead of her, cutting a path for Dana to follow. Within minutes, her feet were frozen and her breathing labored. It took all the energy and will she possessed to keep plowing forward, fighting against the strength of the wind and the bogging weight of the snow. Even as they neared the house, she couldn't seem to summon the strength to run the last few yards. It was Sean who took her wrist, tugging her the remaining few feet.

They stumbled up the stairs and into the foyer, slamming the door behind them. Immediately, the warmer interior caused Dana's extremities to burn and melting snow to drip from her hair and eyelashes. Leaning against the panels, she peeled one mitten free, dropping it to the floor and flexing her fingers. The skin she'd exposed was pink and mottled.

"They're here!" came a cry, and Aunt June ran into the reception area. "They're here!"

She hustled toward them, Mae quickly following, and Aunt April—ever the practical one—bringing up the rear, her arms filled with a stack of towels.

June immediately began to remove their coats and scarves, all the time offering the same sort of babyish prattle she displayed with her dog until April interrupted her, extending the towels.

"Quiet, June."

"But—"

"Let them get their breath." April regarded them through her thick lenses as if looking for signs of obvious injury. "It's about time you got back."

Sean shook his head. "We couldn't get the generator fixed. I don't know what's wrong with it—you'll be needing some new spark plugs before I can check it any farther."

April waved the comment aside. "I doubt that will be happening. Shortly after you left, we discovered the source of the power outage." She fixed a stern gaze on June. "June blew a fuse."

"I was only trying to hang the Chinese lanterns for the ball."

"You could have told someone the lights went off when you plugged them in."

"I didn't think they had anything to do with it."

"Maybe the sparks coming out of the electrical plug should have been your first clue."

June's lips pursed, and her chin elevated as she gave a soft "Humph."

April turned her attention back to Sean and Dana. "You really need to get out of those wet things."

Dana looked at Sean.

He looked at her.

Dana knew they were thinking the same thing. That they would be returning to their room—their *mutual* room—to undress.

A bolt of lightning sizzled through Dana's body, and she wondered how on earth she was going to manage being in close proximity to this man, knowing he was stripping to the skin. How would she manage to keep her hands off him?

"Maybe you should both take a dip in one of the hot tubs," June suggested.

April scowled at her, then thought twice and nodded decisively. "She's got a good idea... for once."

"Really, Aunt April," Dana began. "I don't think—"

"Nonsense. I won't hear another word. You know where the hot tubs are located, Dana. In those little booths right by the pool."

"Yes, but..."

"But what?" April asked as if Dana were arguing a moot point.

"I don't have a suit."

"We'll find you one."

"Sean—"

"We'll loan him Madison's. I'm sure the old man won't mind. I don't think he's worn the thing since we gave it to him last Christmas."

Once again, Dana met Sean's gaze, knowing that he shared her opinion. A hot tub would be no less enticing that being sequestered alone in the honeymoon suite. But how could they possibly refuse without drawing even more attention to themselves.

"Go on, now," April said, nudging Dana in the right direction. "Head on down to the dressing rooms, and we'll see that the suits are delivered."

Since there appeared to be no graceful way to avoid the situation, Dana acquiesced. At least she could take comfort in the fact that any bathing suits her Aunts provided them would be less than titillating.

DANA COULDN'T have been more wrong.

As soon as she heard Aunt April's "Too-da-loo" and unrolled the towel holding the bathing costume, she blanched. But by then, it was too late to protest. Aunt April had gone, taking all of Dana's clothes with her to put in the dryer, and Dana was left with nothing but this. *This!*

She stared in disbelief at the black string bikini, wondering where on earth Aunt April had managed to unearth the thing. It couldn't possibly belong to one of the Flowers sisters. The garment was little more than a few triangular patches of black Lycra held together with the tiniest of strings.

Dana's eyes closed in disbelief.

This had to be a joke. A horrible, horrible joke.

But when she looked again, the bikini hadn't magically transformed into anything other than what it was—a very brief, very dangerous garment.

She met her own gaze in the mirror, seeing the panic. And more. An I-dare-you-Dana kind of expression that she had only experienced a handful of times in her life.

Do it.

Wear the thing.

As soon as the thoughts popped into her head, she pushed them aside, wondering how on earth she could possibly consider slipping into a hot tub with her body barely covered. She'd seen the size of the tubs before—and they weren't really built for more than two people. She was bound to brush against Sean at least once.

Bare skin to bare skin.

Her body began to tremble, and a fireball settled low in her stomach. Moving slowly, almost reluctantly, she stepped into the briefs, then tied the bra around her neck and chest. When she'd finished, she glanced in the mirror. The effect was worse than she'd imagined. Nearly every inch of her body was exposed—and what wasn't open to view was being lovingly hugged by a layer of black ink.

Please, please, she prayed silently. *Let me be the first one into the water.*

But it wasn't to be. As soon as she closed the door to the changing room, she noted that only one of the booths' doors had been left open. Since muted giggles and whispers were coming from the other enclosures, she padded forward to the last tiny cubicle. As she peered inside, she noted a bench, a rack of hooks and Sean O'Malley, who was already neck deep in the bubbling water.

Her fingers clenched the edge of her towel as he opened one eye.

When she didn't immediately move, he asked, "Aren't you getting in?"

"No, I..." But there was no possible excuse for turning tail and running now. Besides, the water looked inviting, so inviting. Almost as much as the glistening shoulders rising out of the bubbles.

"Here, I'll help you."

Then he stood, the water rushing down his body to reveal a microscopic pair of black briefs.

The air rushed from Dana's lungs, and her mouth grew dry. A thudding pounded in her ears, and too late, she realized that it was the thump of her own heart.

"Those belong to Madison?" she finally managed to croak.

Sean was still waiting and he offered her a cock-eyed grin. "I don't even want to think about it."

But the smile disappeared into a heated stare.

"Come into the water, Dana."

She could not refuse. Not when he was studying her as if she were one of the most beautiful women in the world and he the luckiest man.

The towel dropped to the floor at her feet. His eyes flamed. Then he was dragging her to him, lifting her against his chest, his body, kissing her with a passion like none she had ever experienced before.

She moaned, wrapping her arms around his neck, realizing that she didn't really care if they had only known each other for a few short days. Time was irrelevant in matters of the heart. Especially when her soul knew him inside and out. When her body fit against him as if she had finally come home.

Sean slipped into the water, sitting, and Dana straddled his hips with her knees, melting closer and closer, knowing that she needed this man as she had needed no other. He was the yin to her yang, the black to her white.

Her head tilted, and Sean's tongue slipped into her mouth, exploring the honeyed sweetness in a manner that made her weak. She pulled herself even closer, delighting in the sensation of their bodies growing slippery and warm in the water. She could feel his arousal against her, and it thrilled her no end, knowing that she had the power to excite a man like this. Knowing that he wanted her. *Her.*

Her palms swept over his chest, absorbing the firm muscles and the crease that ran down the center of his stomach to his navel, then lower, lower.

He gasped, lifting his head and gulping air into his lungs.

"I think I'm warm enough, are you?"

She couldn't form a coherent word to save her life. "Mm-hmm."

Not waiting for a more formal invitation than that, he lifted her out of the water, cradling her against his chest. Ignoring their robes and the towels, he carried her into the corridor, and from there to the elevator. Only then did he set her on her feet, kissing her even as he reached behind him to push the appropriate button.

The ancient contraption took an eon to make its way to their floor, but neither of them minded. Not when it offered them even more opportunities to kiss and caress, to revel in the passion blazing between them.

As soon as they came to a halt, Sean lifted her again, hurrying down the hall to the honeymoon suite and closing them inside.

Then they were collapsing on the bed in a tangle of arms and legs. Somehow, Dana managed to push Sean's suit over his knees, while Sean quickly divested her of her own swimming gear. Then there was nothing but flesh against flesh.

Dana had long since ceased to think; she could only feel. Feel his warmth settling over her, his breath against her ear as he whispered her name over and over again. Her body was on fire, and her heart was beating an erratic tattoo. For the first time since meeting Sean, she allowed herself free rein to his body, exploring the taut muscles of his shoulders, the crease of his spine, the firm buttocks and powerful legs.

When her fingertips grazed the insides of his thighs, he gasped against her.

"I don't know if I can wait."

"Don't wait. I want you to make love with me. Now. Here."

He needed no further encouragement. His lips closed over her own, and he began to caress her more urgently, more intimately.

Dana became a mass of molten need, of incredible hunger. Passion raged within her like a wildfire out of control. She strained against him, needing to feel his body pressing against hers, rubbing, sliding. When he thrust inside her, there was no fear, no doubt, no hesitation. She knew that she would never regret this moment no matter what the future might bring.

Digging her fingers into the firm muscles of his shoulders, she rocked against him, absorbing the sounds of passion that escaped from his throat. Then she cried out as her body shuddered with the beginnings of its release. Seconds later, just as the man above her reached his own climax, Dana was struck to the core with a staggering thought.

I love him.

She tried to deny the inner epiphany, but it would not go away. And as Sean's body relaxed, growing heavy upon her own, she closed her eyes, knowing that it was true. For the first time in her life, she was experiencing love. Not lust, not mere attraction, not sensual gratification.

Love.

Her fingers slipped into his hair, and she bit her lip, wondering how such a thing could have occurred. But even as a portion of her brain sought to analyze the emotion, Dana decided that she didn't know how it had happened, and she didn't care. All that mattered was that what she was doing was right. So very right.

When Sean rolled away from her, cradling her next to his side, she laid her hand on his stomach, reveling in their closeness—not just physically, but emotionally, spiritually and mentally. At the same time, she prayed that he might some day feel a shred of the same emotion for her. That he might one day fancy himself in love with her, too.

"I'm not sorry," Sean murmured.

She smiled against him at the way he'd felt prodded to apologize. It was such an old-fashioned response. Such a noble one.

Such an endearing one.

"I'm not sorry, either," she responded. "In fact, I'm quite glad we made love."

The room pulsed with an eloquent stillness.

"Dana, I know it has only been a few days, but..."

She placed a finger over his lips. Her own feelings were so new, so fragile, she didn't think she could assimilate anything more. For now, it was enough to lie in his arms and think that someday...

Someday...

"Shh. Not yet," she whispered. "For now, let's just enjoy this."

It was obvious from the tension in his body that he still wanted to speak, but he finally relented, kissing the top of her head. "You're some kind of woman, do you know that?"

A glow settled deep in the regions of her heart. "Yeah. I do."

His chuckle rumbled under her ear.

"But you're some kind of man, too," she finished.

THEY SPENT THE REST of the day in bed, rousing only when Dana's aunts summoned them to the dance marathon to be held that evening.

Dana supposed they must have given every appearance of being a couple in love, swaying cheek to cheek no matter what kind of music was being played, staring deep into one another's eyes, communicating in the way lovers do—without words.

They left hours early, Sean pleading a pulled hamstring. The aunts clucked over the injury—although it was obvious Mae didn't believe such a wound could occur from a slow waltz. But it didn't matter. As soon as the two of them were out of sight of April, Mae and June Flowers—as well as the camera crew—they were running through the corridors to their own room. There, they tumbled onto the bed to make love again and again.

The following day passed in much the same manner. The lazy afternoon was spent alone, walking through the arboretum, playing shuffleboard and helping her aunts to prepare for the grand finale of their birthday celebration. The final ball.

Sean actually started to look forward to the ball— in a way he wouldn't have thought imaginable. Not that he was suddenly crazy about doing the lindy and the jitterbug. No, what he wanted was for this week to be over, the charade to end, the obligations. He needed to have Dana to himself. He needed to get to know her on a more normal footing, without being followed by cameramen or scrutinized by her aunts. He wanted ...

A relationship.

At any other point in his life, the fact that he was actually seeking close emotional ties with a woman would have been astonishing. He would have been the first to admit that he'd been badly burned by his experience with Liz. He'd been young, randy and full of bravado. When the two of them had met, there had been immediate fireworks—and Sean had mistaken those fireworks for love. Eager to do things "right," he'd proposed to her, moved her into his apartment and set up a joint checking account.

The arrangement lasted little more than three months. Within six weeks, they were arguing nonstop. By twelve, they endured each other in icy silence. When Sean came home one day to find his ring in the center of the table and the apartment bare of Liz's things, he had absorbed the sight with a relief like none he'd experienced before or since.

Since then, he'd been suspicious of any sort of passion that flared too quickly.

Until now.

From the onset, there had been a difference between his feelings for Dana and those he'd had for Liz. The passion was there—hotter than anything he'd shared with any woman. But beneath the physical desire was a longing to be with her, to get into her head, to share her secrets.

"Are you ready?"

When Dana's voice came from the other side of the bathroom door, Sean turned from the mirror over the bureau, realizing he'd been staring at his bow tie for the better part of ten minutes.

"Sure. Come on out."

It was a little white lie. He wasn't entirely ready. But he was hoping that Dana would volunteer to fix the blasted thing.

"No."

Her refusal brought his head up, and he wondered if she'd somehow read his thoughts about the tie.

"No, what?"

"No, I'm not coming out."

That remark caused him to cross to the bathroom door. "What's wrong?"

"This dress."

"What about it?"

"Aunt Mae picked it out."

"She has an elegant taste in clothing."

Bizarre and sometimes overly formal, but elegant, he added silently to himself.

"She also has a sick sense of humor."

Now Sean was really intrigued. "Don't tell me the woman offered you a nun's habit?"

"No...."

"Then what could possibly be that bad?"

His only answer was silence.

"Dana?"

He heard a groan from the other side of the door.

"I don't know if I can do this," she wailed.

He propped his hands on the lintel, leaning forward to hear her muttering. "What do you mean?" he asked.

"Let's just say that Aunt Mae must be learning to accept you."

Sean didn't bother to tamp down the self-satisfied grin. "This is sounding better and better."

"That's because you don't have to wear the blasted thing."

"Just come out."

He heard her sigh.

"No laughing," she warned.

"I promise."

"Yeah, I bet."

The knob rattled, and the door eased open with the swiftness of a snail. Since Dana kept her body shielded by the panels, Sean was treated to a mental strip tease of sorts as he tried to imagine all the things Dana could—or could not—be wearing.

But when at long last she stood silhouetted in the threshold, he sucked in his breath.

Aunt Mae was *really* beginning to like him. That was the only explanation possible. Otherwise, she wouldn't have allowed her niece to wear such a thing in front of *him*.

The gown was bias cut, made of a rich, shiny fabric that coated every inch of her body with an elegant black sheen.

"You can't possibly be wearing anything under that," he commented lowly.

"I'm not."

The response sunk like a hot ball deep in his stomach.

"Well, at least not much," she amended.

The dress had a scarflike collar that wrapped around her neck and tied in the back. Below that, a halter bodice cupped her breasts to where the skirt had been attached in an inverted-V shape. From her ribs to her knees, the bias-cut fabric caressed every inch of her body before flaring to the floor and ending in a slight train.

"You're beautiful."

He knew he'd told her such a sentiment more than once, but this time he could think of no other way to say it. Her hair had been drawn away from her face and held there with sparkling combs. Her makeup was subtle and soft except for the deep crimson lipstick she wore.

"I can't believe your aunt ever wore such a thing," he rasped.

"She probably didn't. I had to remove the original tags."

"Why would she buy something and never wear it?"

Dana shrugged. "Why would Aunt June dye Babbette pink?"

"Enough said."

She smiled, touching the rhinestones that studded the collar of the dress, then spread over the bodice like the ever-widening pattern of a rain-dappled spiderweb. "When I originally concocted this scheme, I had Rick pick out some jewelry for an engagement present."

"From me? How thoughtful of you."

She grimaced. "It was a stupid idea—but then, I suppose I went about this whole thing wrong. I hate the fact that I thought it was acceptable to lie."

He wrapped his arms around her shoulders, pulling her close, inhaling the exotic fragrance that clung to her skin.

"Hey, don't be too hard on yourself. If you hadn't been so sneaky and underhanded, we never would have met."

The wry comment made her laugh, and he was glad. He loved to hear her laugh. Loved the way the sound skidded down his spine like the tickle of a finger.

"I have something for you."

He released her, moving the nightstand and opening the top drawer. "Your Aunt April snookered me into playing another round of poker this morning while you were still asleep. After collecting my winnings, I was passing by the gift shop and saw these. They reminded me of you."

He held out the tiny gold box and watched, intrigued as her eyes lit up like a little girl's at Christmas.

"This is for me?"

"Yes. Open it."

There was no shyness in her response. She tugged the ribbon loose, lifted the lid and the layer of cotton padding, then sighed.

"Oh, Sean."

She held the sterling-silver earrings up to the light, watching as the glow played against the oval, faceted garnets in the center.

"They're beautiful," she breathed. "Thank you."

Her arms wrapped around his neck, and she squeezed him tightly.

And at that moment, it was all Sean needed to make him happier than he'd ever been before.

Chapter Ten

The sound of big-band music met their ears yards before they reached the recreation hall. Dana felt the beat fill her very soul, urge her on. Tonight was going to be special. She knew it.

Just before reaching the door, she paused to make sure that Sean's tie was straight.

"You look very handsome in that suit," she commented. She'd always loved a man in a tuxedo, but the period cut, with its wide shoulders and nipped-in waist, was especially flattering to Sean's muscular figure.

"Thank you very much, ma'am." He lifted her hand and kissed the tips of her fingers.

"What's in the box?" he asked, gesturing to the gaily wrapped package.

"English toffee."

His brows rose.

"My aunts have a fondness for a certain brand of British candy. The toffee is soft, more like a caramel, and mixed with dried fruit and nuts. I had a friend who works in London express the stuff to me last week so that it's nice and fresh."

"An unusual gift."

"My aunts are seventy-five years old. When a person gets to that age, a new teapot seems to be a little superfluous. Besides, I learned long ago that my aunts are very sentimental. They appreciate the thought of a gift much more than the price."

"Very wise ladies."

They made their way into the midst of the party—and even Dana, who had been a part of the preparations, had to gasp in delight.

A mirror-covered ball had been suspended from the ceiling. Multicolored spotlights dappled the floor with color. Paper streamers and balloons and linen-covered tables had been augmented with bits and pieces of memorabilia collected from the Flowers' U.S.O. travels.

"It's fantastic," Dana breathed, heading for the reception line.

"Your aunts do have a knack for the dramatic."

The aunts stood near a punch fountain, welcoming their guests and accepting the pretty birthday packages being given them.

"Dana, you look wonderful!" June exclaimed as soon as she saw her niece. "And Sean! My, how you fill out a suit!"

Dana expected Sean to grow stiff and uncomfortable, but he only laughed.

"You're always good for my ego, Aunt June."

Aunt June. The familiar term sounded so good coming from his lips.

April took the present and shook it. "Toffee!"

The other aunts beamed. Even Babbette—who had been groomed with curling ribbons and a jeweled sweater to match June's evening gown—sniffed at the box and wriggled in delight.

"You always know just what to give us, don't you, dear?" June murmured. "Mae, is that one of your dresses?"

Mae nodded, but she was looking at Sean. "What do you think of it, Mr. O'Malley?"

She still wasn't calling him by his first name, but Dana was relieved that she wasn't referring to him as Ramone any more.

"I think it's wonderful, Aunt Mae. You have a flawless eye for fashion."

Aunt Mae's lips cracked into the slightest of smiles.

"Go on, you two," April urged. "Go start the dancing."

Sean didn't seem to need a second urging. He led Dana onto the polished dais that had been set up in the center of the floor.

They took their position of honor beneath the spinning ball just as the taped orchestra began a rendition of "Satin Doll."

"Very appropriate," Sean murmured next to her ear.

"Mm-hmm." She wasn't really thinking about that. She was thinking more about the feel of him against her. The fabric of her dress was sliding against her skin with each step, creating a very erotic sensation. It was enough to make Dana think that the "good old days" hadn't been as prim and proper as she'd always believed.

"What are you thinking about?"

Dana smiled, allowing her fingertips to dip into the collar of his shirt.

"I don't think I'll tell you. Not yet. It could make dancing very difficult for the next few hours."

"How so?"

"We wouldn't be able to sit down. Your suit might be cut quite comfortably, but there are limits to how much a pair of trousers can—"

"Say no more." The command was low, husky and filled with a latent promise. "We'll continue this discussion later."

She hoped so. She truly hoped so.

"SEAN?"

Sean glanced up at the elderly woman who hovered next to his chair. Martha. He thought that was her name. She was a mean poker player with a gambler's knack at bluffing.

"Yes?"

"You had a call come through the front desk. I think it's important."

She handed him a scrap of pink paper and withdrew.

Sean took one look at the sheet, and the bottom dropped out of his stomach.

"Excuse me," he said abruptly.

He didn't even wait for an acknowledgment from Dana or her aunts, but rushed out of the room. Heading to the bank of phones by the registration desk, he quickly dialed his home phone, waiting impatiently as it rang on the other end.

"Come on, Carol, come on," he murmured to himself, knowing that if Carol was calling from Cache Valley rather than her own apartment, something was seriously wrong.

"Hello!" The greeting was frantic.

"Carol? It's Sean."

"Sean..." His name was interrupted by a sob. "Sean, they're going to take them away."

"What?" Sean covered one ear to muffle the big-band music, sure he hadn't heard Carol correctly.

"They're going to take the babies away. Social services made a surprise visit..."

She started to cry, and Sean squeezed his eyes closed, praying that Carol was jumping to conclusions.

"Carol? Carol," he called, trying to calm her. "Take a deep breath and tell me what happened."

He heard a sniffle, muffled talk, then the clatter of the phone. When he heard a voice again, it wasn't Carol, but Mary-Kate.

"Sean?"

"Yeah. What's going on?"

"It's been horrible here—worse than it ever was after you did that calendar. Ever since the news of that auction hit the television stations, we've had a herd of women camped out on our doorstep. Not just those groupies that we had before, but reporters and photographers. We tried to get them to go away, but it got to the point that we just barricaded ourselves in the house. Aunt Madge and Uncle John saw the commercials and decided to come check on things. As soon as they saw the mess, they forced the authorities to make a decision. The judge has ruled that—as things are—our home is an 'unfit environment for minors of this tender age.'"

With each word, Sean's mouth was growing more and more dry and his stomach began to churn.

"Get a hold of—"

"No, Sean. They've already handed us the documents. Aunt Madge is in the other room packing their things. They're taking them today. Now."

Sean's hand balled into a fist, and he pounded the wall, swallowing the curse that bubbled into his throat.

Was that how it was going to end? Were his little sisters going to be taken away from them all so quickly, so irretrievably, without Sean's having a chance to explain his side of things?

"Sean?"

He pulled his attention back with sheer strength of will. "Yeah. I'm here."

"When will you be home?"

The query was so soft, so forlorn, he felt as if his heart were being torn from his breast.

"Tomorrow."

"But—"

"I'll be there tomorrow, Mary-Kate. Don't worry. Don't do anything rash. Aunt Madge has to stay in the area for at least a day or two. I'll see if I can't straighten things out."

"Okay." Again, the note of defeat, of infinite sadness.

"Bye, Mary-Kate. Tell everyone I love them."

It was the same way he'd ended every phone call for as long as he could remember, but this time, it seemed to hold far more meaning than it ever had before.

Sean reluctantly terminated the connection and stood for several seconds, his hands propped on the counter, his head bowed.

Damn it.

Damn it all to hell and back.

He couldn't even imagine what life at the O'Malley house would be like without Ellen, Marcia and Deborah. They were so much a part of them. They were the primary reasons why the older O'Malleys had been able to continue with something akin to a normal life. They were the reason Santa Claus still visited, the Easter Bunny, the tooth fairy... They were the reason Sean didn't spend eighteen hours a day on the job. He loved to come home to find the living-room floor scattered with toys and crayons. They were the reasons he made a weekly trip to the library for picture books and Saturday-afternoon runs to the doughnut shop.

What was he going to do?

The thought had barely had the chance to ricochet through his head when the normal party sounds were split by a horrible scream.

Sean's head shot up, and without thought he began running toward the recreation hall. Serving as a volunteer fireman had taught him the significance of certain sounds. There were screams of rage, delight and fear. But this had been a scream of pain.

As soon as he entered the darkened room, he immediately saw the knot of people clustered around the refreshment table.

"Somebody call an ambulance!"

"The roads are still closed."

"A doctor. Is there a doctor here?"

When Sean recognized the last voice as Dana's, it made him cringe.

"Step back, please, coming through."

As if he were Moses, the sea of people parted, allowing him to join the group huddled on the floor. Dana was kneeling over one of the aunts, and as he came closer, he realized April was sprawled by the refreshment table.

"What happened?" he asked as he knelt beside them.

Dana's face was pale. "She slipped on some spilt punch. I think she's broken an ankle."

"Ohhhh," April moaned, gripping at Sean's jacket. "Help me. Please, help me."

The weak, quavering voice was so unlike April that Sean took her hand.

"Don't worry, Aunt April. I'll take care of you."

"Are you a doctor?" Mae asked.

June elbowed her in the ribs. "He's a rancher. We already know that much, Mae."

"But—"

"He must have done this with a cow or something."

Dana shot them a quick glance. "I told you he was a fireman."

"I have some EMT training," Sean said quickly. "Does the village have any first-aid supplies?"

Mae nodded. "I'll go get them." She poked the elderly man at her side. "Madison, come with me."

Sean gestured to the rest of the gawkers. "I need you all to give April some air. In fact, it would be better all the way around if you headed into the reception room until we're done here."

There was a murmuring, some words of encouragement, then they melted into the hall.

"Dana, can you find a way to shut off the music?"

She nodded, then disappeared through a far door.

As soon as she'd disappeared, April clutched at Sean's lapels. "Am I going to die?"

He was already working his way down to the injured ankle. "I doubt if this will prove fatal, April."

She tugged at his jacket, preventing him from moving any farther.

"Listen to me.... If I die..."

"You're not going to die."

"But if I do...I want you to know that I think you're a wonderful man. So polite. So good-natured."

"Thank you."

"No, really. I think you're the best thing to ever happen to my niece."

Sean couldn't speak past the knot in his throat.

"I'm glad you'll be marrying her."

"Aunt April..."

She gripped his hand. "Please, tell me you'll take care of her."

He felt an invisible hand gripping his chest.

"Please, Sean. Tell me you'll do it."

Mae chose that moment to return, running into the room with Madison in tow.

"Here's the kit!"

Sean had never been so glad to see anyone in his entire life.

As he opened the oversize tackle box filled with medical paraphernalia, he was pleased to see that it was well stocked.

"We also sent for Mort the mortician," Mae gasped, breathless from her rush. "He'll bring a gurney to transport her."

"Good."

After a few minutes, Sean was able to determine that the ankle wasn't broken. There was no swelling as yet, so he was sure it was a mild sprain, but with a seventy-five year old woman, he supposed that there really wasn't any such thing as a mild injury.

"Did you hit your head as you fell, April?"

She moaned.

"There might be a possibility of a concussion, so I think that someone should stay with you tonight. As soon as the storm clears, we'll send for a doctor."

She snagged his wrist. "Will you stay with me, Sean? You and Dana?"

He wanted to refuse. Right now, his nerves were strung tighter than a bowstring, but he didn't know how he could say no. Not while staring into bright blue eyes magnified three times their size by April's glasses.

"All right. We'll stay with you."

Mort rattled into the room with his gurney, and Sean carefully lifted April's frail body, setting it on the mattress. "I'll see you upstairs."

She seemed ready to grab him by the coat tails—quite literally—but Mort began to wheel her away. He must have been intent on crashing some sort of sound barrier, because he careered into the corridor in the direction of the elevator, her sisters toddling close behind.

"Will she be all right?" The question, weak and full of fear, came from directly behind him. He turned to see Dana clenching and unclenching her hands.

"I tried to get hold of a doctor," she said.

"Good thinking."

"Not really. They still won't allow any traffic on the roads unless it's a serious emergency." She hesitated before asking, "*Is* it a serious emergency?"

"I doubt it. But we'll keep our eyes on her."

Her head dipped to show she understood. "I did receive word from the sheriff that he'll stop by early tomorrow morning. If we need to take her to the hospital, he'll transport us then."

"Good." Sean paused, ready to tell her that he would be leaving, too, that he had to get home, but he couldn't. He couldn't bring himself to say the words.

The silence became thick and heavy, but to Sean's infinite sadness, it was not the comfortable quiet that they had shared only hours before. He kept thinking about his sisters. Hordes of reporters on his doorstep. And April. Poor April. The old woman thought Sean was really going to become a member of the family.

"Dana..." The question he'd been about to ask stuck in his throat. "Dana, I need to know something."

"Aunt April—"

"This doesn't have anything to do with your aunt. This is about the interview you scheduled for tomorrow."

Her brow furrowed. "What about it?"

"I, uh... There's been a bit of a crisis at home, and I've got to be leaving as soon as possible."

"Yes, of course." The words were matter-of-fact, but it was obvious that she didn't completely understand.

"Dana, did you advertise the interview?" He had to know. He had to know if it was because of her that his home had been besieged.

"My station did, yes. It's part of the package."

He'd been expecting her to admit such a thing, but even so, knowing her actions had led to the reversal of his guardianship didn't make his chest feel any lighter.

"Sean? What's wrong?"

She reached out to him, but he neatly sidestepped her, not sure what he was supposed to feel, how he was supposed to act. All he knew was that he'd lost something in the past hour. Something bright and fragile and precious.

Trust?

Perhaps.

Ardor?

No, that burned as bright as ever.

"Let's go upstairs," he finally said.

There would be plenty of time to think about what to do next, he decided. All the time in the world.

SOMETHING WAS WRONG with Sean. Dana knew it. She could see the tension etched on his features, the stiff set to his shoulders, the far-off stare of his eyes. But he wouldn't confide in her—he wouldn't even talk. Instead, he'd slouched in one corner of Aunt April's sofa and had turned on the television.

Even that was a pretense. She knew he wasn't paying attention. For the past two hours, he'd been watching a documentary on bees being narrated by a very nasal-toned British announcer. Yet when Dana had asked him a question, Sean hadn't had a clue why drones were called drones.

"It's been a couple of hours," she announced needlessly. When Sean would have risen, she shook her head. "I'll go wake Aunt April and check on her."

Sighing, she moved into the bedroom with its beige chenille bedspread and tan scatter rugs. She'd tiptoed the entire way to the bed, but when the lamp on the nightstand flipped on, she realized she needn't have bothered. Aunt April was already awake.

"Are you in pain?" Dana asked, concerned.

April ignored the question, patting the side of her bed. "Come sit down."

Dana immediately complied, taking a spot that was as familiar to her as the faint scents of cigarillo smoke and lilac water that invariably clung to Aunt April's skin.

"Sean told me to ask your name, rank and serial number to ensure you were lucid," she informed her aunt.

"Cheeky devil." But there was a fondness to the reply. "I'm as fit as a fiddle. I've lived in this rickety old body long enough to know when I'm sick."

"Even so, only a few hours ago, you were talking about dying. I think we should take you to the doctor as soon as we can, just to make sure."

Aunt April pooh-poohed the idea, but when Dana made it clear that she wouldn't be backing down, she finally ceased her complaining.

The two of them settled into the pillows just as they had a hundred times before when April had read Dana bedtime stories.

"You know," April said after some time, "that Sean of yours does remind me of Ramone."

"Aunt April," Dana protested.

"No, really. Ramone was a wonderful man."

"He was romancing all three of you at once."

"Ah," she drawled. "But that's where you are wrong." April took a deep breath, closing her eyes halfway as if looking into another time. "It was after the war, you know. There were still troops being shipped back home, so we were sent to Dover to entertain our American boys and keep them from getting too restless. The first time I saw Ramone—" she took a deep breath "—I thought he was a god."

"Aunt April..."

"No, really. He was tall, handsome, with wicked eyes and a smile that could light up a room. All it took was a single glance, and I knew I was in love."

Dana regarded April suspiciously, wondering if this were some new sort of fairy tale.

"I'd been around my share of show-business men before—and you grow wary of the type. But Ramone was different. His sophistication was only skin-deep. Beneath it all was an earthiness, a primal passion."

Dana couldn't speak. She'd never heard April talk like this before.

"That's when it all started, I suppose."

"What?"

"The misunderstanding." April's eyes opened. "I wasn't the first one to fall in love with him at first sight. Mae caught a glance of him at about the same moment and all but claimed him for herself. She set her hopes on that man."

"In what way?"

"No matter what she might say or how she might act now, Mae hated show business. She was so sure that Ramone would fall madly in love with her and take her away from it all. Deep in her heart, I think the only thing she ever wanted was to be a wife and mother." She sighed. "Unfortunately, Ramone loved me."

Dana refrained from commenting, sure that she would hear the same statement from each of the triplets if she bothered to ask.

April must have sensed her thoughts because she laughed. "Reach into that nightstand."

Dana did as she was told.

"There, under the scarves."

What she found was a stack of letters tied with a frayed pink ribbon. Dana didn't recognize the handwriting, but she could see that the paper was old and worn as if it had been handled time and time again.

"Those are the love letters he gave me. We had a passionate affair, Ramone and I, but I was so afraid of how our romance might hurt Mae—she's always been such a fragile creature. I encouraged him to be nice to my sisters, to dazzle them with compliments and special attention. Ramone agreed, reluctantly, but after several months, it soon became obvious that Mae was growing almost... obsessed with the man. Ramone grew tired of the game and begged me to return with him to Cuba. To be his wife."

"What happened?" Dana asked, absently stroking the letters.

April's chest expanded with a heavy sigh. "I said no. I couldn't do that to Mae. It would have devastated her. I didn't have the heart to choose the love of a man over the love of my family."

Her gnarled fingers plucked at the bedclothes. "I regretted that decision for years. Looking back, I think that Mae would have understood eventually. It might even have forced Mae and June to find husbands of their own. Instead, with that single refusal, I established a pattern. The three of us would stay together. Always. There would never be a man alive who could split us up.''

"Oh, Aunt April," Dana murmured.

April sniffed and wriggled a bit. "Well, it's no use fussing about it now. What's done, is done, as they say. But I told you the truth for a reason, not just to hear myself ramble.''

She took Dana's hand, squeezing her fingers. "Dana, I want you to promise me that if you love this man, really love him, that nothing June, Mae or I say will matter. Family is family. They have to love you. But a man... Well, if you have the love of a man, it's not something to give away lightly.''

Dana felt her throat tighten. Leaning over, she pressed a kiss to April's cheek.

"Thank you, Aunt April."

April patted her arm. "Now, go into the other room and tell that nice young man how much I've grown to like him, you hear?''

"Yes, Aunt April."

SEAN COULD HEAR the voices in the bedroom, but not clearly enough to understand what was being said—and for some reason, he felt a sadness creep into his body.

He'd been resistant to the Flowers triplets when he'd first met them, but he had to admit that he'd grown fond of them. He'd even grown to enjoy their eccentric ways. But he couldn't let himself think about that. Not now. Not when his family was about to be split in two.

His fingers curled into fists again, and he fought to stay in control, but no matter how hard he tried to ignore the issue at hand, his mind kept returning to one point.

Dana Shaw had put him back in the public eye.

And it was that public scrutiny that had caused him to lose his sisters.

Resting his head against the back of the couch, he willed himself to remain calm, to think things through. Grasping the remote, he flipped through the channels, not really seeing the images on the screen, but knowing he had to do something, anything, to divert his attention.

Then he caught sight of his own face.

Returning to Channel 9, he watched in ever-dawning horror as a close-up of his calendar shot was displayed. The voice-over was going on and on about "local sex symbols" and "bachelors for hire." Then the date and time for the broadcast of tomorrow's interview flashed across the screen.

Although the commercial was only thirty seconds long, by the time it finished, Sean felt as if he'd been stripped naked. Emotionally and physically.

A slight noise made him turn, and he saw that Dana had joined him. She was staring at the television in horror.

"I guess you didn't want me to see that," he commented, a cold anger beginning to push away his despair. He automatically punched the Power button.

"I did not write that copy."

"Sure." The word was rife with sarcasm. Sean pushed himself to his feet and was halfway to the door when she stopped him.

"I swear to you, I did not write that copy. That commercial is obscene."

He clenched his teeth together to summon his control, then asked, "Why didn't you tell me you'd be advertising the interview?"

"I assumed you knew."

"You assumed wrong."

She offered a short sigh. "Look, I'm sorry about that...that...trash," she said, gesturing to the television set. "I'll find out who's responsible and give them a piece of my mind. But what's done, is done."

He offered a short bark of laughter. "Yeah. It's done. For the past week, that commercial has been aired in front of my family, my associates and my community. By the time I get home, I'll be labeled as some stud for hire."

She huffed in indignation. "I think you're exaggerating the situation."

"Am I?"

He opened his mouth to say more, then shook his head and exhaled. "I'm going to bed."

He didn't wait for her response. He merely strode into the hall, slamming the door behind him.

Tonight, he would sleep in the honeymoon suite alone.

Chapter Eleven

The next morning, Dana found Sean in the sun room just off the dining hall. He was standing with his feet braced apart, the tips of his fingers tucked into his pockets. On the floor beside him, she saw the familiar duffel bag and his coat.

"Hi," she murmured, slipping her arms around his waist and kissing his back. She hoped that if she reacted as if nothing had happened the night before, they could get back on an even keel. "How was your rest?"

Sean didn't answer her. He was carefully studying something out the window.

Tipping sideways, Dana peered around him, blinking at the dazzling light. Mother Nature, ever fickle, ever changeable, had decided that there had been enough bad weather. A clear blue sky hung like a blue glass bowl over the craggy mountain range. Wind-sculpted drifts sparkled beneath the buttery warmth, beckoning for someone—anyone—to come outside and spoil the perfect drifts with footprints or a snow angel.

Chuckling, Dana caught sight of a line of elderly Greycliff residents heading into the forest on cross-country skis, binoculars slung around their necks and haversacks strapped to their backs.

"That's the bird-watching group. They're probably off searching for wildlife in the woods."

But when she stepped to Sean's side, ready to share her joy at the beautiful morning, it was to find Sean staring at her with hard eyes.

"I have to give you credit, Dana. When you want an interview, you'll do anything you have to in order to make sure it goes according to plan."

Dana's mouth opened at the sudden attack. "What?"

He bent to scoop up a newspaper that had been lying on the chair. It was folded in such a way that she couldn't avoid the advertisement for her upcoming special. Taking precedence over the copy was a full-size reproduction of Sean's calendar shot.

"Don't play the innocent," he growled. "You knew I was growing to care for you. You knew I was beginning to look upon our relationship as being personal rather than professional. And you couldn't let that happen, could you? Because to you, it was all a game."

He planted his hands on his hips, staring up at the ceiling as if mentally tamping down his anger. "Tell me, how long did you think it would take me to figure out that all of those accidents were staged?"

"I don't understand." Dana's lips had grown so stiff, she didn't know how she managed to force the words out.

"Come, now. You can't possibly think that I'm going to ignore everything you've done. The way you arranged for the elevator to stall so that you could pump me for information—not just once, but twice."

"I did no such thing!"

"Did you rig the blown fuse, too? The shared room? Your aunt's fall?"

She gasped, unable to believe that he could accuse her of such things.

"What about the lovemaking? Was that all an act, too?"

Dana wasn't even aware that she'd moved until she heard the crack of her hand slapping his cheek.

Sean grasped her elbow when she would have stormed past him.

"Well?"

She refused to dignify such a question with an answer, so she said instead, "Consider your services paid in full, Mr. O'Malley. You are free to go anywhere you'd damn well like. I'll call the sheriff and tell him you'll be needing a ride into town, if that's what you want."

Dana would have thought he'd jump at the offer, but he was shaking his head. "Oh, no, Ms. Shaw.

You wanted an interview, so you're about to get it. I won't have you saying later that I reneged on the deal."

"I told you—"

"And I told you. I'll fulfill my bargain—every last detail. Then I'll be heading home."

When he released her and left the room, Dana thought she was going to fall to the floor. Her knees were trembling and her stomach roiling, but propping her hand against the wall, she forced herself to breathe. In and out, in and out. She wouldn't think of what had happened, wouldn't think of the ugly things they'd said to each another.

She turned, leaning against the sideboard where the phone was located, about to call the station and demand information on who was responsible for the advertisement. It was then that her eyes slowly focused on a tiny scrap of crumpled paper on the floor.

She wasn't really conscious of moving. She only knew that she was unfolding the slip, smoothing out the wrinkles and reading the simple scrawl: "Carol called. Publicity has swayed opinion. Babies will be going to Aunt Madge."

The nausea in her stomach increased. It didn't take a crystal ball to decipher the cryptic message. Sean had just been informed that he'd been denied custody of his sisters. And what had swayed the decision was the publicity he'd received at Dana's request.

Sinking into a chair, she rubbed the blinding ache settling into the back of her head. Shame consumed her. What had she done? How could she have been so selfish? Sean had told her of his struggles to maintain custody of his three little sisters, but it hadn't even dawned on her that by pursuing her own objectives, Dana could put such a plan in jeopardy.

It was all her fault.

Her fault.

Shoving the paper into her pocket, she ran into the recreation room, intent on pulling him aside and apologizing, but when she saw the way he waited in one of the chairs set up for the interview, she wondered what she could say. All the explanations, all the apologies, wouldn't help him in the least. The decision had been made.

Sean O'Malley had lost what he'd loved most.

And because of that, she'd lost Sean O'Malley.

She gazed at him, willing him to turn to meet her eyes, but he focused his attention on the cameramen.

"Hey, Westman. Let's get this over with," he prodded Adam.

Adam shot him a thumbs-up sign. "Whenever you're ready, Dana."

But Dana couldn't even think, let alone hold an interview. She was far too conscious of the waves of hostility and resentment ebbing her way from where Sean sat only a foot away. But that foot may as well have been a mile.

Finally, her professionalism kicked in. Taking her seat, she clipped on her microphone. When the time came, she found herself smiling and looking into the camera just as she'd done a hundred times before.

"Good afternoon," she said since the piece would be aired just before the five-o'clock news. "Welcome to this week's edition of 'Utah People.' Today, I'm pleased to announce that we have a special guest. You've heard of him, you've probably seen his picture, but this afternoon, you're about to learn what kind of man lies behind the calendar. Mr. Sean O'Malley."

She waited a beat for a close-up to be taken of her guest.

Her guest?

Her lover.

"Mr. O'Malley, I'm sure that our audience is intrigued at how a rancher from Cache Valley, Utah, ended up as Mr. January for the 1995 Volunteer of the Month Calendar. How exactly did that happen?"

Sean's eyes were so dark, they were nearly black. "I was asked."

Dana waited for him to elaborate, smiling encouragingly, but it soon became apparent that he didn't plan to say anything more.

"Who was it that asked you?"

"The firemen's auxiliary."

Again, she waited.

Again, there was no elaboration.

"Was this something you'd ever considered doing before?"

"No."

Silence. Dana could feel a faint heat gathering in the hollow of her back and under her arms.

"And what was the purpose for your doing it, then?"

"A new roof."

"For?"

"The fire station."

"I see. And how was the reaction in your community when the calendar came out?"

"Awful."

"In what way?"

He leaned forward, and she didn't entirely like the gleam that entered his eyes. "Strange women began following me around, trying to get my number, trying to get my address. Some nut-case even stole my dry cleaning so that she could call me to come and claim it."

"And did you?"

"No."

"So am I to understand you weren't entirely comfortable with the publicity you received?"

"Hell, no."

Dana was sure a hint of pink was beginning to seep into her cheeks.

"So if you were so uncomfortable with everything that occurred, why did you arrange to serve as one of the bachelors for the Make a Wish Foundation auction?''

"I didn't volunteer. It was my sisters' strange way of getting me a date for New Year's Eve. They thought I'd appreciate the joke.''

"I see.''

"Do you mind if I ask a question, Ms. Shaw?''

Dana was stunned. The person being interviewed was not supposed to reverse the roles.

"Why did *you* bid on me?''

Now she knew her cheeks were bright red.

"Make a Wish is one of my favorite charities,'' she said breezily.

"But why did you bid on *me?*''

How was she supposed to answer that? If she said it was for professional reasons, he would think she'd done it for the interview alone. If she said it was for personal reasons, he would probably blurt to the world that she'd wanted to introduce him as her fiancé to her eccentric aunts.

"I think we're getting a little off the subject here,'' she said, deciding it would be wise to dodge the issue altogether. "I'm sure that many people would like to know more about you. Such as where you live.''

"Paradise.''

Her mouth opened, and she floundered for a reply. "Pardon?''

"I live in Paradise. It's a few miles south of Logan.''

"Ah," she drawled, realizing he hadn't been toying with her.

"You've mentioned that you make your living as a rancher."

"Beef," he interrupted before she could ask.

"How m—"

"Two thousand head."

She couldn't help it. Her jaw dropped. Two thousand? *Two thousand?*

"And you oversee this by yourself?"

"I've got help."

"Your family?"

"No."

So they were back to the gunshot answers.

"That must be a very lonely occupation when compared to...say, someone who works in an office."

His eyes narrowed ever so slightly. "Not at all. When you trust the people you work with, honestly care for them, it makes things a whole lot easier. Don't you think trust is important, Ms. Shaw? Don't you think that a person's integrity should be taken into consideration at all times?"

He may as well have flashed a sign saying We're Finished, Dana. At that moment, with that veiled response to her queries, she knew there would be no explanations, no going back.

Dana wanted to weep. She could feel the tears at the back of her throat, working their way up, but she summoned every last ounce of will she possessed and pasted a bright smile on her face.

"We'll be right back after this commercial break."

THE REST OF THE INTERVIEW steadily deteriorated. By the time they'd finished and the cameras had been turned off, Dana's head was pounding and her jaw felt as if it would shatter from the way she'd clenched her teeth together.

Unhooking her microphone, she stood, holding out her hand.

Sean looked at it for a moment, but didn't take it.

"I know you don't believe me," she said slowly, "but this isn't the way I wanted things to happen."

He didn't respond, and she couldn't think of anything else to say. She'd known him too short a time to know how to break through his stormy silence.

Without a word, he brushed past her, she supposed to gather his things.

Making her way outside to the portico, Dana leaned her shoulder against one of the supports, bowing her head to keep anyone from looking too closely at her face. She knew she should probably take this opportunity to make a clean getaway, but she found she couldn't do that yet. She had to watch him go. She had to know that he wouldn't give her another chance to explain.

Several times, she heard the door open and close. On each occasion, she stiffened, digging her toe into the snow beneath her feet in a show of nonchalance, but it was only a few of the guests departing, then her aunts, who had bundled into their finest coats to bid their friends goodbye. Hearing the cheery farewells, the kissing and laughing and teasing rejoinders, Dana curled her hands into fists, praying she could endure it all. Just a little longer.

Just a little longer.

Then the door opened behind her, and she knew in an instant that it was Sean. Knew it by the electricity that thrummed between them, the way each nerve in her body stood at attention. She felt the way he paused, the way he looked at her, then the thump of his boots on the portico.

He didn't pause, didn't even say goodbye, and that hurt more than anything else.

"Sean?"

Dana cursed herself for calling out to him, but she couldn't seem to help herself.

"Sean, I'm sorry."

He didn't acknowledge that he'd even heard.

"If I'd had any idea that the interview could hurt your chances at keeping the family together..."

He glanced at her over his shoulder, and at that moment, beneath the anger in his eyes, she saw a pain equal to her own.

"Goodbye, Dana."

The way he said her name, slowly, the syllables lingering on his tongue, brought to mind visions of laughter and intimacy and lovemaking. She wished she had the courage to run toward him and throw her arms around his neck. Any other person would beg him to stay. Beg him to give her another chance. Beg him to love her.

But Dana didn't know how to beg.

She wasn't even sure if she knew how to *love*. Not the way this man deserved to be loved. By a woman who had old-fashioned values. Who would bake him cookies and call him snookums.

"Bye, Sean," she whispered.

Then he was gone.

Leaving her heart aching and hollow.

Chapter Twelve

Her aunts joined her on the porch, watching as Sean folded his lean form into the passenger side of the Jeep.

"Where's he going?" April demanded.

"Home," Dana said forlornly. His home. Someplace far away from her.

The roar of the engine sounded very loud in the post-storm stillness. Then the tires skidded, held, and the vehicle began its descent to the highway.

"Why's he leaving with the sheriff?" June asked.

"Because he doesn't want to see me again." Dana's throat tightened unbearably. "He doesn't even want to ride in the same car as me."

April made a tsking sound. "It's a shame."

June took a handkerchief from her pocket. "Terrible."

Mae sighed, "I really liked the man."

Dana regarded her aunts in disbelief. "But you hated him. All of you!"

April shook her head. "That's not true, dear. We always liked him. All of us."

"He was perfect for you," June lamented.

"Absolutely perfect," Mae echoed.

Dana's mouth dropped. She couldn't help it. "Then why have you all been so...so...?"

"Disapproving?" April filled in.

"Contrary?" June added.

"Stubborn?" Mae quipped.

"Yes!"

April patted her on the arm as if it were fine with them that Dana was being particularly dense.

"We had to be that way, Dana."

"If we hadn't," June said, "you wouldn't have been nearly as attracted to him."

"There's something about a hard-won fight that makes the prize that much more worthwhile," Mae continued knowingly.

A slow horror was beginning to flood Dana's system. "You mean all of this, this whole week, was an act?"

April squeezed her elbow. "Of course it was—well, most of it, anyway. We knew that you were planning to pass him off as some sort of 'significant other' the moment we saw that woman's report on the television."

Dana was thoroughly confused now. "What woman?"

"That Jeanine what's-her-name from that other channel."

"You've been watching the competition?" Dana demanded, wondering why—after all she'd been told—that piece of information was equally disturbing.

"We like to keep informed."

"What does that have to do with me?"

Mae's expression became smug. "I told you she didn't know that Jeanine woman closed one of the newscasts with the information that Dana Shaw had spent fifteen hundred dollars at a bachelor auction."

"Really, Dana," April chided. "You could have been a little more fiscally responsible."

"Personally, I think it was a bargain," June said, her eyes twinkling knowingly.

"Anyway," April continued, "we had a feeling you would be bringing him to our birthday party."

June grinned. "So we planned this whole elaborate scheme—even all that nonsense about Mae's thinking he was Ramone—to make you that much more determined to prove us wrong."

"Then we orchestrated all those accidents—the elevator, the power outage, the faulty snowmobile—to give you some time together," Mae confided.

"But..." The question Dana had been about to ask faded into silence.

It didn't really matter what her aunts had or hadn't done. The fact remained: Sean didn't trust her. He thought she'd purposely destroyed his chances for him to keep his sisters together.

April hugged her close. "We're sorry, Dana. I suppose we went overboard with our plans. What can we do to help, hmm?"

Dana wanted to accept their offer. She wanted to believe that there was something they could do to fix things. But deep down, she knew it was impossible. Only one person could do that.

And that was Dana.

As soon as Dana arrived in Salt Lake City, she scrubbed the interview taken with Sean at Greycliff, citing technical problems with the tape. Her superiors at the station were far from pleased, but when they realized that they would be able to advertise the segment even more, they reluctantly acquiesced.

Immediately, Dana took charge of reorganizing the commercials and ads. Then she made arrangements for Rick and Adam to journey to Paradise. Making up some excuse as to why she couldn't go herself, she instructed them to meet with Mary-Kate O'Malley. After speaking with the woman and explaining her relationship with Sean, the mistakes she'd made and her motives for wanting to help him, Dana had arranged for the girl to gather home footage of Sean's real life—the hard work involved with ranching and the heartache in serving as his sisters' only parent.

Sending one of her interns to Cache Valley, she instructed her to interview friends and neighbors who knew him well, fellow firemen and the Scouts whom he'd taught CPR.

As soon as they'd returned, she spent hour upon hour putting together a comprehensive view of this complicated man. One who had been thrust into the limelight through his efforts to help the community and who now regretted his loss of privacy. She even touched on the death of his mother and the condition of his father. She gave an overview of how he'd fought to keep his family together—and how the publicity garnered by the results of the bachelor auction had endangered those attempts. Through it all, she hoped she'd given an honest account of Sean's dignity, humor and loyalty.

Two weeks later, on the night the piece aired, Dana took personal leave, sitting in front of the television, watching, waiting. As soon as the program ended, she huddled on the corner of the couch, expecting some sort of call, some sort of response.

Two hours later, she realized that—other than her aunts—there would be no contact.

Not from Sean O'Malley.

Still, she prayed that she would hear from him. Maybe tomorrow.

Twenty-four hours later, she returned from work and nearly ran to the answering machine. A light blinked, urging her on. But when she played the message and discovered that no one but a phone-survey service had called, she burst into tears.

Sean O'Malley hated her.

She would never hear his voice again.

THE RINGING OF THE PHONE jarred Dana from a depression-induced sleep. Rubbing her eyes, she peered at the clock. Eight in the evening. She'd been asleep for less than fifteen minutes. Fifteen minutes in nearly two days.

Automatically, she reached for the receiver, praying it wasn't some emergency call from work. She'd taken a week's vacation, citing personal reasons, but the truth of the matter was that she couldn't face the real world yet. She'd gone into seclusion, spending most of her day in bed, alternately torturing herself with watching game shows and talk shows and sobbing as if her heart would break.

"Hello," she croaked, automatically poking at the carton of Baskin-Robbins hand-packed ice cream she'd set on the nightstand.

"Hello, sweetie!"

Aunt April.

"Hello, Aunt April."

"Listen, I only have a minute—water aerobics are about to start. I was supposed to call and tell you that one of your dear aunts has arranged for an escort to drop by this evening."

"Aunt April—"

"It isn't me, hon. I tried to talk her out of it, but she wouldn't see reason. Be nice to the man, Dana. After all, I doubt he's to blame for your troubles."

Then there was a click, and the line was disconnected. Almost simultaneously, the doorbell rang.

Dana dropped her head onto the bed, hoping, praying, that it wasn't true. It couldn't be true. Her aunts couldn't be matchmaking again.

Ring.

Damn.

Dana rolled from the bed, marching into the living room. Damn it all to hell and back. When she'd told her aunts that she'd wanted some time alone, that was exactly what she'd meant. She wanted time *alone.*

To recuperate.

Brood.

Stew.

The closer she got to the door, the hotter her anger burned. She'd bet fifty dollars that she knew just who was responsible for this particular evening's escort. Aunt Mae. The woman couldn't accept the fact that Dana had no romance in her life. Perhaps she wanted to show Dana that Sean *had* been just like Ramone.

A cad.

A rounder.

A rake.

Deciding that she wasn't about to give the man any sort of encouragement at all, Dana didn't even reach for the robe she'd left on the dining-room chair. Whoever was on the other side of that door was going to see just what it meant to spend the evening with Dana Shaw on a night like tonight. It meant the glamorous newscaster he'd been told would be his escort had gone into hiding. In her place was a woman teetering in the edge of manic depression. A woman who had been in her pajamas the better part of a day, hadn't combed her hair since she'd scooped it into an untidy ponytail and had been eating ice cream straight from the carton.

The bell pealed again, and she swore loud enough to be heard on the other side, flipped the dead bolt and yanked the door open.

"What!" The very rude, very abrupt demand burst from her lips before she even had a chance to focus on who might be waiting. When her eyes transmitted the information to her brain, she stood rooted to the spot.

Sean.

Sean O'Malley.

As well as Rick Bermen and Adam Westman from Channel 9.

She automatically touched her hair, then grabbed at the placket of her pajamas.

"What do you want?" she grumbled, wondering how her heart could ache so much just at the sight of Sean.

"May I come in?"

She took one look at the cameras and shook her head, remembering the way she'd left her kitchen, her living room. The word *pigsty* wouldn't do the mess justice. "No."

One of Sean's eyebrows rose at the response, but he didn't seem nearly as upset as he should have been. In fact, he looked slightly amused. Too late, she wondered if she had fudge-ripple ice cream smeared all over her face.

Hiding the carton behind her back, she closed the door as much as she could, peering out of the slit she'd created.

"This might go a little better somewhere other than the hall, Dana."

She sniffed. "That's too bad."

Again, the twitch of his lips. "Okay..." he drawled. "We'll do it here."

When he dropped to one knee, Dana stared at him, wondering what was going on and why the cameras were so intent on every move.

"What are they doing here?" she asked, pointing to his companions.

"We've bonded."

"Since when?"

"Since I decided I don't give a hoot in hell how we met...as long as we did."

Her brow furrowed. "What have you been drinking, Sean O'Malley?"

She heard a snicker coming from Adam's direction.

"Nothing."

"Then why are you slinking around on the floor."

"I'm not slinking. I'm kneeling."

"Same thing."

"Not quite."

She sighed. "Fine. Have it your way. Just tell me what you want and get out of here before my date arrives."

For the first time, she saw his smile falter.

"Date?"

She shrugged. "I'm sure my aunts have something planned for me this evening."

His good will returned. "Yes, I suppose they do."

Reaching into his jacket pocket, he removed a tiny box.

"Dana LaRee Shaw—"

"How did you find out my middle name?" she growled. She hated that name. It sounded so...so...spinsterish.

Which, she supposed, was an accurate description of the kind of woman she was doomed to be in the future, she thought with an inner sniff.

"Dana, would you hold your tongue and let me get this out?"

"Fine." She pressed her lips together.

"Dana LaRee Shaw. During the week we spent together—"

When her mouth opened, he held up a silencing finger.

"During that week, I had the pleasure of getting to know you in a way I've never known another woman."

She glanced at the cameras, hoping to heaven that the true interpretation of that remark wasn't about to be transmitted to the world.

"At first, I was irritated—"

Again, she opened her mouth.

Again, he stopped her.

"But my irritation soon faded to fascination."

Fascination?

"Unfortunately, instead of looking at what was right beneath my nose, I let myself be sidetracked by frustration and anger."

She made a sound that sounded very much like an I-told-you-so snort.

"But after only a few days apart, I realized that I don't want to spend another day without you."

It took a moment for the words to sink in. When they did, her body began to tremble, and she found herself looking from Sean, to the little box, to the camera crew.

"Oh, my gosh," she breathed, her stomach doing flip-flops.

"Dana, I have a very special question I need to ask you."

"Wait. Wait!" She held up a hand, tried to speak, but couldn't. "Just wait," she whispered, then slammed the door in his face, running through the apartment to her bedroom. Ripping the pajamas from her body, she stepped into a pair of black slacks and a sweater. Dodging to the bathroom, she combed her hair, quickly slapped on the minimum amount of cosmetics needed to make her appear humanlike, then dragged a comb through her hair. She was running through the dining room when she had to rush back and brush her teeth. Then, vaulting over a stack of magazines, she zipped through the living room and whipped the door open again.

"Okay," she said breathlessly.

Sean was standing, talking in a low voice to the cameramen. When he turned and saw that she'd changed her clothing, his expression lightened.

"You had to change your clothes?" he asked in disbelief.

"I couldn't let you propose to me with ice cream on my face, could I?"

He grinned, sauntering toward her with that cat-like confidence she would associate with him for the rest of her life.

"You still have ice cream on your face," he murmured, kissing her cheek, her lips, her chin, with such thoroughness, she was sure that ice cream had only been an excuse.

"Are you ready now, Ms. Shaw?"

She nodded, clasping her fingers together.

"Dana LaRee—"

"Aren't you going to kneel?"

He sank to the ground. "Dana LaRee—"

"Yes!"

"To what?"

"Yes, I'll marry you."

A tightness gripped her throat when she saw the way he looked at her then. As if she were the only woman on earth. As if she were the center of his universe.

At that moment, she knew the extent of his love, and the power it had over her was astounding, exhilarating and humbling all at the same time. This man adored her. He worshiped her. But not as a man might revere an idol. No, he regarded her as the most intimate of friends, the most complete of lovers.

Unable to stand even the slight distance that remained between them, she fell into his arms, trying to apologize for all that had transpired, all the mistakes that had been made.

Vaguely, she saw him wave the cameramen away as he whispered in her ear, "There is nothing to forgive, Dana. We belong together. It only took me this long to realize that fact."

"But your family. I almost—"

"Shh. Everything is fine. My sisters are still with us—due in part to the information you put on the air about how I was trying to keep all of us together. My aunt backed away from taking them. She said anyone who would go to the lengths of auctioning his services for charity in order to keep his family whole deserved her support, not her defiance."

"Oh, Sean . . ." It was all she could manage to say around the knot in her throat.

"I want to marry you, Dana," he murmured. "I want to marry you so much I ache with it, but you have to know up front that my sisters come along as part of the bargain."

"I don't care."

"As a rancher, I've got long hours."

"So what?"

"And I want kids and a mortgage and everything else that marriage entails."

"That sounds wonderful," she breathed, cutting off anything else he might say with a long, slow kiss.

"So you'll have me, hmm?" he asked when they finally parted.

"As long as you realize I'm a rotten cook," she said fearfully.

"I can cook."

"You should also know that I'll probably never call you snookums."

He laughed at that response. "Why would I want you to?" He leaned close, whispering in her ear. "Just call me husband. Lover. Could you do that?"

She nodded, wondering how he could think she might refuse. This man had won her respect and her admiration. Her heart and her soul. Her mind and her body. In the short time she'd known him, he'd given her untold joy and ecstasy. And from now on, although women might stare his way or envy her for snaring herself a walking, talking calendar man . . .

The only arms allowed to hold him would be her own.

"I love you, Sean O'Malley," she breathed against his lips.

"And I love you . . . Mrs. soon-to-be-O'Malley."

It was the nicest thing anyone had ever called her.

AMERICAN ❖ ROMANCE®

The Randall Brothers—living out there on their Wyoming ranch with only each other, their ranch hands and the cattle for company.... Well, it could make a body yearn for female companionship! Much as they miss womenfolk, these four cowboys don't cotton to being roped and branded in matrimony! But then big brother Jake brings home four of the most beautiful "fillies."

Don't miss what happens next to

Chad—COWBOY CUPID October '96

Pete—COWBOY DADDY November '96

Brett—COWBOY GROOM January '97

Jake—COWBOY SURRENDER February '97

4 Brides
for 4 Brothers

They give new meaning to the term "gettin' hitched"!

Heartbreak RANCH

Four generations of independent women…
Four heartwarming, romantic stories of the West…
Four incredible authors…

Fern Michaels
Jill Marie Landis
Dorsey Kelley
Chelley Kitzmiller

Saddle up with Heartbreak Ranch, an outstanding
Western collection that will take you on a whirlwind
trip through four generations and the exciting,
romantic adventures of four strong women who
have inherited the ranch from Bella Duprey,
famed Barbary Coast madam.

Available in March,
wherever Harlequin books are sold.

HARLEQUIN ®

HTBK

AMERICAN ROMANCE®

What's a woman to do when she hasn't got a date for New Year's Eve? *Buy* a man, that's what!

And make sure it's one of the eligible

That's exactly what friends Dana Shaw and Elise Allen do in the hilarious New Year's Bachelors duet. But the men they get give these women even more than they bargained for!

Don't miss:

#662 DANA & THE CALENDAR MAN
by Lisa Bingham
January 1997

#666 ELISE & THE HOTSHOT LAWYER
by Emily Dalton
February 1997

Ring in the New Year with NEW YEAR'S BACHELORS!

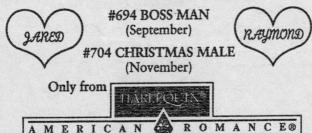

Harlequin and Silhouette celebrate
Black History Month with seven terrific titles,
featuring the all-new *Fever Rising*
by Maggie Ferguson
(Harlequin Intrigue #408) and
A Family Wedding by Angela Benson
(Silhouette Special Edition #1085)!

Also available are:
Looks Are Deceiving by Maggie Ferguson
Crime of Passion by Maggie Ferguson
Adam and Eva by Sandra Kitt
Unforgivable by Joyce McGill
Blood Sympathy by Reginald Hill

On sale in January at your favorite
Harlequin and Silhouette retail outlet.

Look us up on-line at: http://www.romance.net   BHM297

FREE
VALENTINE'S
BROOCH!
$9.95 U.S.
retail value

This Valentine's Day Harlequin brings you
all the essentials—romance, chocolate
and jewelry—in:

VALENTINE
Delights

Matchmaking chocolate-shop owner Papa Valentine
dispenses sinful desserts, mouth-watering
chocolates…and advice to the lovelorn, in this
collection of three delightfully romantic stories
by Meryl Sawyer, Kate Hoffmann and Gina Wilkins.

As our special Valentine's Day gift to you, each copy
of *Valentine Delights* will have a beautiful, filigreed,
heart-shaped brooch attached to the cover.

Make this your most delicious Valentine's Day
ever with *Valentine Delights!*

Available in February wherever
Harlequin books are sold.

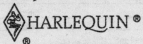

HARLEQUIN ®
®

Look us up on-line at: http://www.romance.net

VAL97

HARLEQUIN®

Don't miss these Harlequin favorites by some of our most distinguished authors!
And now, you can receive a discount by ordering two or more titles!

HT#25645	THREE GROOMS AND A WIFE by JoAnn Ross	$3.25 U.S. $3.75 CAN.	☐
HT#25647	NOT THIS GUY by Glenda Sanders	$3.25 U.S. $3.75 CAN.	☐
HP#11725	THE WRONG KIND OF WIFE by Roberta Leigh	$3.25 U.S. $3.75 CAN.	☐
HP#11755	TIGER EYES by Robyn Donald	$3.25 U.S. $3.75 CAN.	☐
HR#03416	A WIFE IN WAITING by Jessica Steele	$3.25 U.S. $3.75 CAN.	☐
HR#03419	KIT AND THE COWBOY by Rebecca Winters	$3.25 U.S. $3.75 CAN.	☐
HS#70622	KIM & THE COWBOY by Margot Dalton	$3.50 U.S. $3.99 CAN.	☐
HS#70642	MONDAY'S CHILD by Janice Kaiser	$3.75 U.S. $4.25 CAN.	☐
HI#22342	BABY VS. THE BAR by M.J. Rodgers	$3.50 U.S. $3.99 CAN.	☐
HI#22382	SEE ME IN YOUR DREAMS by Patricia Rosemoor	$3.75 U.S. $4.25 CAN.	☐
HAR#16538	KISSED BY THE SEA by Rebecca Flanders	$3.50 U.S. $3.99 CAN.	☐
HAR#16603	MOMMY ON BOARD by Muriel Jensen	$3.50 U.S. $3.99 CAN.	☐
HH#28885	DESERT ROGUE by Erine Yorke	$4.50 U.S. $4.99 CAN.	☐
HH#28911	THE NORMAN'S HEART by Margaret Moore	$4.50 U.S. $4.99 CAN.	☐

(limited quantities available on certain titles)

	AMOUNT	$
DEDUCT:	**10% DISCOUNT FOR 2+ BOOKS**	$
ADD:	**POSTAGE & HANDLING**	$
	($1.00 for one book, 50¢ for each additional)	
	APPLICABLE TAXES*	$_____
	TOTAL PAYABLE	$_____
	(check or money order—please do not send cash)	

To order, complete this form and send it, along with a check or money order for the total above, payable to Harlequin Books, to: **In the U.S.:** 3010 Walden Avenue, P.O. Box 9047, Buffalo, NY 14269-9047; **In Canada:** P.O. Box 613, Fort Erie, Ontario, L2A 5X3.

Name:_____

Address:_____ City:_____

State/Prov.:_____ Zip/Postal Code:_____

*New York residents remit applicable sales taxes.
 Canadian residents remit applicable GST and provincial taxes.
Look us up on-line at: http://www.romance.net

HBACK-JM4